Murder by the Spoonful

(An Antique Hunters Mystery)

by

Vicki Vass

Copyright 2015 by Vicki Vass

For information, email **Cozy Cat Press**, cozycatpress@aol.com or visit our website at: www.cozycatpress.com

COZY CAT
P R E S S

ISBN: 978-1-939816-67-2

Printed in the United States of America

Cover design by Paula Ellenberger
http://www.paulaellenberger.com/

1 2 3 4 5 6 7 8 9 10

To my dear friends—Anne, CC, and Betsy. Thank you for inspiring me every day. A special thank you to "the pants" for making this story possible. And to my husband, Brian, for sharing the journey with me.

This book is dedicated to June Tedeschi.

Chapter One

"Sybil!" Anne called out, feeling the crunch of breaking glass under her feet. Family photos lay silent on the entryway tile floor looking back up at her. "Sybil!" she called again, with increasing urgency. There was no reply. Faded imprints of where the images had hung lined the narrow hallway walls. With every step Anne took, the ghostly remnants dabbed at the painting that was forming in her mind.

When she reached the living room, the painting was complete. Screaming, she took a step back, stumbled and fell to the floor, landing face to face with Great-Aunt Sybil.

Later, waiting for the police to arrive, Anne paced up and down the front porch. She wanted to run but she didn't want to leave Sybil alone. She scanned the front yard to see if she'd missed anything. There was nothing, other than the broken leaded glass window on the front door. After seeing her aunt's body, Anne hadn't had the courage to walk around the rest of the home. Her first inclination had been to bolt. That wasn't right. She owed it to Aunt Sybil to find out what had happened. She sat down in the Victorian rocking chair and nervously chewed her fingernails. Aunt Sybil would smack her on the back of her head if she saw her biting her nails. It was a childhood habit that she'd long outgrown. She didn't care much for manicures or spending money on frivolous pampering. Twenty-five dollars could buy more important things like vintage hatboxes, antique perfume bottles or heirloom postcards.

It had been a while since she'd visited her Great-Aunt Sybil. *Great* was a title not an adjective used to describe her aunt Sybil. Her age and her wealth entitled her to speak her mind, which estranged her from the rest of the Hillstrom family. Like most of the Hillstroms, Sybil had emigrated from Sweden when she was a little girl. Sybil was the keeper of the Hillstrom family archive. That was the purpose of Anne's visit today—the Hillstrom family bible.

Anne remembered playing on this porch as a child, and it hadn't changed since then. Two white wicker Victorian rocking chairs graced the front porch—one empty. She admired the Chinese jardinière pot on the bronze stand in the corner. She hadn't seen it before. She wondered if Aunt Sybil would mind if she took it with her. She had just the spot. . . *What am I thinking? Sybil's dead.*

A handsome young man walked up the stairs and stood in front of Anne, breaking her trance. "I'm Detective Charlie Johnson of the Glencoe Police Department. You're Anne Hillstrom?" He looked down at the small notebook in his hand.

Anne stood up and nodded.

"Your aunt is inside?" the detective asked.

"Yes, in the living room."

A pair of EMTs ran past the detective into the house. Anne watched, knowing their attempts would be futile. She'd seen enough CSI to know that Sybil was gone.

The detective returned shortly and sat in the rocker next to Anne. Seeing that she was noticeably upset, he placed a hand on hers as he spoke. "Do you need us to call someone for you? Are you okay?" he asked in a calming voice.

Anne thought for a moment. Her list of go-to I-C-E (in case of emergency) contacts was short. It made her sad to think about it. She looked up at the detective, teary eyed. "What happened? Why did this happen?"

The detective asked, "Did you notice if anything was missing?"

Anne looked back at the Chinese jardinière pot. She was relieved that it was still there. "I can make a list of what I believe is missing."

"Do you know anyone who would want to harm your aunt?"

This list in Anne's head was much longer than her list of friends. Sybil was not well loved. "Do you think it was intentional?"

"We're not ruling anything out," Detective Johnson said.

A deluge of mourners poured in from around the Midwest. Grieving third cousins from Minnesota, distraught sisters in-law from Milwaukee, Hillstroms, Holmes, Hellfrims—all manner of kin gathered to pay their final respects to their much beloved, although seldom visited, Sybil Hillstrom. Anne didn't recognize most of them.

The relatives hadn't been much help over the past few days. Anne had made all the arrangements not only for Sybil's service but also for her out-of-town visitors. Per her final request, Sybil was laid to rest in an open casket to display her beautiful jewelry. Sybil was dressed in the height of 1940's fashion, wearing her satin ivory wedding dress and adorned with the most precious jewel of her collection—a diamond and emerald brooch once owned by a Swedish Viking queen. She'd never had the chance to wear the wedding dress in life but now she would wear it in death. The brooch and any hope that the Hillstroms held of owning it, was being buried with Sybil. It was her last chance to thumb her nose at her greedy relatives. Anne managed a small smile as she watched the cavalcade parade past, shedding their crocodile tears. One by one they filed out of the small chapel heading to the adjacent gravesite.

After the room had cleared, Anne was left with one final moment alone to say a private goodbye to Sybil. Then the funeral director closed the casket with a click. As Sybil was carried to the gravesite, a choir sang, "How Great Thou Art." After the pallbearers had gone, Anne sank down on one of the folding chairs in front of where the casket had been and took her shoes off.

Around her, Anne could hear a relative whisper, "I heard she hid a fortune somewhere in the house."

"I can't believe she let Sybil be buried in that brooch," Anne heard her cousin Suzanne's husband, Jack, whisper behind her.

"Ssh," Suzanne murmured, clutching the hand of one fidgeting child while holding the other on her lap.

Anne hadn't seen her cousin in a few years and couldn't believe how much she'd aged. Born three months apart, Suzanne had been her constant companion growing up. Now she looked ten years older, thanks to two kids and Jack.

Hearing similar whispers swirling around her, Anne strained hard to hear something nice, anything nice, about Great-Aunt Sybil.

Anne had loved Sybil in spite of her ornery disposition or maybe because of it. Although they hadn't seen each other in years, she knew that Sybil loved her as much as Sybil could feel love. They'd shared a passion for collecting old things, treasured trophies, needful things, or as Sybil would put it "orphaned artifacts."

That probably explained why Sybil had named Anne executor—a role that Anne had been glad to fill.

The coffin began its descent into the freshly dug grave. Its passenger, Sybil Hillstrom, had spent a lifetime collecting other people's memories. Now she was a memory herself, a part of the collection of memories buried in Chicago's Graceland Cemetery, along with others with names like McCormick, Armour, Pinkerton and Burnham.

Anne dropped the single white rose onto her great aunt's coffin. Behind her, CC put her hand on Anne's shoulder.

Great-Aunt Sybil disappeared into the dirt and along with her the identity of her killer.

Chapter Two

CC Muller sat on the Chicago commuter train heading back to the western suburbs. It had been a long day full of late-breaking news, deadlines and interviews. She looked up from her iPad and caught a good-looking man giving her a quick glance and a smile. He was dressed in blue jeans and a sports jacket. She looked him over with her journalistic eye. His salt and pepper hair was a little too long for a business executive and, with his dark tan, he obviously worked outside most days. He looked comfortable in the jeans but not the sports jacket as he pulled and tugged at it. He probably didn't wear a jacket on a daily basis.

Not bad, she thought. Here she was turning 40, and she was still turning heads. The time she put in at the gym seemed to pay off. It wasn't like she was training for the Olympics, but she was in good shape. Kickboxing, spinning, yoga—she did them all. It was the divorcee work-out plan.

After fifteen years of taking care of someone else, she had finally made time to take care of herself. Fine cooking, excellent wines, extensive traveling, good books and good friends. She was comfortable with living on her own and who she was becoming. She took a second glance at the man on the train as she flipped her short brown hair over her shoulder.

The train stopped with a jerk at the Glen Ellyn station. She put away her iPad. Standing up, she brushed against the man who smiled at her. Her way of thanking him for the attention. As she walked out the train doors, she promised herself she wouldn't turn around but she didn't keep her promise. For a split second, their eyes locked, and she felt sixteen again. And then the man on the train was gone.

Chapter Three

Anne pulled up in front of her two-car detached garage. Her 1992 Mercury Mystique was filled with everything she could rescue from Aunt Sybil's house before the estate sale.

Jan Kustodia, known to the neighborhood as Grandma Jan, was waiting for her in the driveway. She'd just brought Anne's garbage cans up from the curb. Anne had forgotten it was garbage day. At 75-years-old and 90 pounds, Grandma Jan had more energy than Anne could muster. She was the neighborhood watch dog and advocate for Linden Avenue. If it happened on Linden Avenue, Jan knew about it.

Jan waved as Anne climbed out of the car. "Anne, how are you?"

"I'm good, Jan. I was cleaning out Aunt Sybil's house."

Grandma Jan walked over to the overfilled car and took a peek inside. "Can I help you carry this in?"

Anne paused. She was exhausted but couldn't bring herself to let Jan see her garage because she knew Jan would want to clean it. "No, I'm good. I want to take my time and go through things."

"I've made some Italian wedding cookies for you. I usually wait until spring to make them because the oil stinks up the house. I left a plate by your front door," Jan said.

Anne had told her a thousand times that she was on a low carb diet, but Jan was old school Italian. Low carb meant only two helpings of pasta. "Thanks, Jan."

"We're having a meeting next week about the streetlights. I talked to the Alderman and as long as we get enough signatures they're going to put in new streetlights. I'm heading to the meeting after Bunco tonight." Bunco was Grandma Jan's only vice. It was the geriatric equivalent of craps. Jan touched Anne's arm. "Listen, dear, I know you've been through a lot. I want to let you know I'm here if you need me. I'll keep an eye on things if you need to spend more time at your aunt's."

"Thanks, Jan," Anne said, giving her a congenial smile. She waited for Jan to walk away before reaching into her car and pulling the trunk lever.

Opening the trunk, Anne reached in and shifted the overflowing contents. She pulled out a moving carton filled to the brim with a copper kettle, a Longaberger basket and a collection of ten ruby-colored sherbet glasses wrapped in newspaper. The burglars had no clue as to the value of these antiques—not monetary value, but of the sentimental value they had to Anne.

Sybil had left her most precious possessions to Anne. The copper kettle had been owned by Sir Arthur Conan Doyle, who'd made his tea in the pot while writing Sherlock Holmes. In the backseat was the stoneware pickle crock that Sybil's father, Booty Hillstrom, had brought with him from Sweden. She pulled both the crock and the box it was in out of the car and set them to one side.

Anne removed a four foot by six foot section of wood from the trunk. She admired the varnished maple planks inlaid with ebony darts. Of all of Sybil's possessions, this was her most cherished. Built in the 1930s, the Belmont Avenue bowling alley was a

Chicago landmark. When the bowling alley closed in the 1970s, Sybil was able to buy this section of one lane. It was the place of their last date before her fiancé shipped out in 1944. He never came home, and Sybil never loved again.

Struggling with its weight, Anne dragged it behind her, scraping up the blacktop driveway leading to the garage, which was her staging area. Inside was an accumulation of years of hunting and gathering. She stopped to wipe her brow. Anne caught her breath. *Maybe she should move the treadmill into the house,* she thought. Then she continued on. Laying the wood down at the entrance of her warehouse, she looked for a safe spot for Sybil's items.

In one corner was the baby buggy from her childhood, in another corner was an abandoned pedestal sink. Holding center stage was the waterfall bureau, dresser, and bed frame from her grandparents. Pots and pails. Ladders and lanterns. Basically anything that didn't fit in her rented storage units wound up in the garage before making its way to the big house.

She placed the wood floor section in the garage and then added the box and the crock. Closing the overhead door, she carried the copper teakettle into the house. Her white Persian Sassy was waiting by the door. Following Anne into the kitchen, Sassy sprung onto the table, touching down lightly, then catapulting up onto the shelf above. The cat wound her way around the heavy antique coffee grinders like a slalom racer. She perched on the edge of the shelf, the best vantage point to watch the opening of the can. Anne felt the eyes of the furry gargoyle piercing through her. Sassy sat perfectly still waiting for the right moment to pounce. At the sound of the electric can opener, Sassy leaped from her perch, nearly knocking over a solid brass Peruvian grinder.

After she ate, Sassy thanked Anne for dinner by rubbing her soft freshly cleaned fur against her leg. Anne filled the copper kettle with water and placed it on the stove. She opened the refrigerator and stared at the cottage cheese, but grabbed an oversized chocolate muffin. The kettle made a mournful cry as steam rose from its spout. *Its previous owner was dead,* Anne thought, now the kettle was an orphaned artifact. "Orphaned artifact," she said out loud, "that's what Aunt Sybil called them."

Chapter Four

The sun sparkled off Lake Michigan. The drive from Chicago up Sheridan Road meandered through forest preserves bordered with giant old-growth poplars and evergreens. Each turn through the winding road gave a peek at the beautiful great lake.

CC and Anne talked of daily events, of pleasantries that good friends often share. But Anne's mind drifted. She thought about what she might find at the estate sale they were heading to in the prestigious North Shore suburb of Kenilworth. Old money, old homes and lots of old treasure.

"What was that?" Anne asked coming out of her trance.

"You didn't hear a word I said, did you, Anne?" CC said with a giggle. She knew her friend well enough to know that her thoughts were elsewhere. "Have you heard from the Glencoe police?" CC repeated.

"I haven't heard anything. I took over a list of what I knew was missing last week. They have no new information or at least that's what they said," Anne said.

"Do they believe it was a robbery that went bad?"

"You know as much as I do. There were no fingerprints or evidence. And, there have been no other break ins in the area." Anne's mood had dampened.

"I'm sorry, Anne. I didn't mean to upset you." CC patted Anne's leg.

They arrived at the mansion at eight a.m.—an hour before the sale was scheduled to begin. The iron gates at the end of the road were open, and the circle drive in front was already packed with cars. CC parked on the shoulder, narrowly missing the bumper of a white Cadillac Escalade. The home was modeled after an English country estate with its brick exterior clad in green ivy. The center of the circle driveway featured a water fountain with a six-foot tall statue of Neptune, who bore a striking resemblance to the owner of the estate, Tim Whitmore.

Getting out of the car, Anne recognized the periwinkle blue Aston Martin coupe that held the pole position. It belonged to Betsy Buttersworth, no relation to the syrup, but still a sticky problem for Anne. She was Anne's Professor Moriarty, her long-time estate sale nemesis. Betsy was a skilled antique hunter and had the money to back up her bids.

Anne ran to the front of the line to grab numbers for herself and CC. She hoped they'd be in the first wave of the assault. They waited for the massive 500-year-old monastery double doors to open. She saw Betsy clutching her Hermès purse, *last year's model*, she thought. Both women wore their battle faces. For Betsy, antique hunting was a distraction in what was just another boring day. For Anne, it was a chance to touch history.

The doors opened wide, and Mr. Ripley stepped out calling numbers. As always, he conducted himself with an old world manner and introduced himself as Alexander Ripley of Ripley Antiquities. Quite tall and handsome, Anne often wondered if some of the ladies came for him as much as for the sale. His pencil-thin mustache reminded Anne of Douglas Fairbanks. He always dressed in vintage Armani and always wore a white carnation in his lapel.

Walking single file, Anne and CC handed him their numbers. Mr. Ripley paused for a moment and held

Anne's hand. "Thank you for coming. I was so sad to hear about your aunt. She was a good friend for many years. I'll personally handle the sale," he said.

"Thank you. That means a lot to the family," Anne said, removing her hand, anxious to get into the house. Anne and CC entered the majestic hallway, which soared three stories encompassing the double winding marble staircase. A Swarovski crystal chandelier hung from the high ceiling. It glittered in the morning sunlight that was crashing through palladium windows. The late Tim Whitmore, owner of this beautiful estate, had been dirt poor until he won the Illinois Powerball. *Apparently money could buy good taste,* Anne thought.

"I'm so excited," she said. "This is going to be good. Look at this, CC." Anne picked up a moonglow-glazed Van Briggle art pottery vase from a console table in the hallway. A hallmark of the arts and crafts era, the vase was a signed piece by artist Van Briggle, the "Lorelei" vase was an excellent example of the Colorado studio's work. She looked at the hefty price tag and set it down immediately. It was too rich for her wallet. She'd recently seen one appraised in the tens of thousands of dollars.

Anne followed CC into the living room. She stopped to inspect and pick up each item, oohing and ahhing as she went. She was in her element. Entering the dining room, she was transfixed by a place setting of china. She sat in a Hitchcock chair by the table and picked up the plate to confirm the name on the bottom. English bone china, she was correct. She'd never seen this pattern, which depicted a hummingbird on a pink and gray background. Anne could hear the one-way strains of Betsy's phone conversation as she walked by, her arms overflowing with crystal candlesticks, a Lladro, and a small pale pink vase.

"I'm going into the basement," CC said from behind her. Anne knew she hoped to discover a collection of tools. Whitmore had been a mechanic before he was a millionaire.

"I'll meet you down there," Anne said. "I'm going to look upstairs first." She stood and headed up the winding marble staircase, passing under the watchful eyes of Degas ballerinas. She paused, eyeing them. They were excellent examples of the Impressionist's work. They were all marked "NFS," meaning *not for sale*. *Figures*, Anne thought, even though she knew she could never afford one. "NFS" was her least favorite acronym.

She wandered through the upstairs hallway, pausing to look at a pile of plush towels in the guest bathroom, stopping in a bedroom to peruse the books on the shelf. She peeked in what appeared to be the master bedroom. A sign on the door said "Do Not Enter," which made Anne want to enter even more. Looking over her shoulder, she tiptoed in. The walls were painted dark maroon, the four-poster bed had to be as big as two king-sized beds, but it was the only thing of any value in the room. Over the fireplace, there was an autographed poster of Richard Petty in his NASCAR uniform, and on the mantle was a tower of beer cans including Pabst Blue Ribbon, Old Style, and Colt 45. This room didn't have the panache or elegance of an interior decorator's touch as did the rest of the house. It must have been Tim's refuge. It displayed his southern Illinois roots with its giant-screen TV, Barcalounger and a large faux leopard skin rug. Everything from his pre-millionaire life appeared to have been dumped into this room. *No wonder this is off limits*, Anne thought. *There's nothing in here but junk. Not worth buying.*

Her eyes drifted to the nightstand. *What is that?* she thought, looking at a crystal ashtray. When she bent down to take a better look, she noticed something underneath the bed. She checked behind her, making sure the coast was clear. None of the items in this room had price stickers, but then again none had "NFS" stickers either. She reached under the bed and retrieved what appeared to be a tattered linen pouch.

Looking inside, she found a tarnished ornate teaspoon with some stray tea leaves stuck inside. The scent from the English breakfast blend was overpowering but what really caught her attention was the spoon itself. It was pretty beat up but still worthy of her own collection. Spoons were one of her weaknesses. She knew she had to have it. Taking the spoon out, she returned the pouch to its hiding place.

Back downstairs, she brought the spoon over to the woman who was helping Mr. Ripley. She was busy ringing up purchases, so she looked very quickly at the spoon and said, "$5."

"Can you please hold it for me while I look around a little more?" Anne asked.

After wandering through the rest of the house, she met up with CC in the basement. CC's arms were filled with industrial supplies like boxes of bolts, copper wire and a socket set. She was most excited about what she'd found deep in the corner of the basement—a 1950's Rolleiflex 3.5F.

She showed it to Anne and explained, "This is a TLR, a twin-lens reflex camera. It uses two lenses—one at the top to focus. All the best press photographers used it in the 1950s. It's German precision at its best, Anne." CC thought of herself as an artist over a vast array of mediums, including photography, oil painting and scrapbooking.

Anne had many of CC's photographs—most of her subjects were missing the tops of their heads. Anne wasn't sure if that was a statement or poor photography.

She suspected the latter but didn't want to hurt her friend's feelings. "That's great, CC."

"You know I've been wanting to add a darkroom. I have to make room in my craft room. Are you ready to go?" CC asked.

"I think I'm done. I found a spoon; they're holding it for me." Anne was also carrying a hand-embroidered tea towel, a white ceramic bulldog and a green Depression-era glass vase. Anne tapped her foot impatiently waiting for the assistant to ring up her items. She was done here and anxious to move on to the next sale.

The woman turned to Anne, jotted down the prices for her purchases on a pad of paper. Anne scrounged in her purse and dug out some wadded up dollar bills. The woman very carefully wrapped her finds in newspaper and plastic bags and waited for CC to pay.

Anne and CC walked out of the house and back to CC's 10-year-old Pontiac Grand Am and headed into the city.

Feeling satisfied with their day's purchases, they stopped for lunch at one of their favorite spots. CC and Anne sat in a quaint little French Bistro overlooking Lake Michigan.

When the waiter came over, CC ordered in French while pointing at various items on the menu. The waiter nodded, even though he obviously didn't speak French.

The two best friends enjoyed a lovely meal on a lovely afternoon—that would change their lives forever.

Chapter Five

CC arrived at her three-bedroom split-level home situated on a large lot in unincorporated Glen Ellyn. After the divorce, she'd done a lot of remodeling. Getting rid of her ex-husband was the first step. The deer heads and pinball machines followed. Thank God for Craig's List. Opening the door, Bandit, her Australian shepherd, nearly knocked her over.

"Hey, boo boo bear," she said, petting his soft brown and white fur. "How's my baby?" She gave him a hug. Bandit's tailless butt rpm'd at an incredible speed whenever CC was near. "Let's go for a walkie, and then we'll figure out dinner."

Putting on the dog's leash, they headed the short distance to the Prairie Path, the former site of an electric railway that extended 61 miles from Chicago to far western Elgin and Aurora. It had been transformed into a bike path in the early 1960s. The lilacs released an intoxicating fragrance as they walked down the gravel pathway. CC pondered the day's events while Bandit caught bees. He wrangled a big fat bumblebee, shaking his head as it stung him. He still looked quite satisfied with his catch.

Daffodils, irises and crocuses were in full bloom. It was one of CC's and Bandit's favorite places to walk. It gave her a chance to think about her blog and gave Bandit a chance to take in the smells. It also gave her a chance to test the new camera. She stopped along the way and took photos of the blooming flowers.

After a brisk 30-minute walk, it was time to head back to the house for dinner. She entered the backyard through the tall, cedar gate. It was a large backyard, nearly an acre. Living in unincorporated Glen Ellyn had its benefits. She'd had to give up city water and sewer but it was worth it to have such a large landscape to decorate. She stopped to pull out a few weeds in her vegetable garden. *A couple more weeks*, she thought, *and she should start seeing growth*. Bandit bumped her leg with his head. It was way past dinnertime. "Ok, Bandit, we'll head in. I promise," she said.

She opened the sliding door into her sunroom and followed the dog into the house. This was her second favorite room after the kitchen. The large travertine tile floor and wood-beamed ceiling made a cozy place to sit in all four seasons. After John had left, she'd installed a Ben Franklin stove in the corner for winter evenings. She was proud of that stove and her newfound skills. She'd learned how to do a lot in the last five years. She took a last glance out the sunroom window into her garden, pleased with its progress. The harsh winter had killed some of her weeping cherry trees and her favorite butterfly bush, but the rest had fared pretty well. Bandit prodded her again. "Ok, boy, dinner's coming," she said, walking into her gourmet kitchen.

This was the first room she'd remodeled. She loved to cook, and she loved to eat. CC was a true foodie. She especially loved French and Creole cuisine. Her parents had emigrated from Germany when she was very young and had settled in La Place, Louisiana, where her dad had worked at the steel mill. That's where she'd fallen in love with spicy food and the steel industry.

She put a frying pan on the stove, chopped some garlic, onion and rosemary, and put it in the pan with some lemon-infused olive oil. She went to the pantry and took out a Mason jar which contained a spicy blend from last year's peppers and tossed some in the pan. She took two chicken breasts from the sub-zero and threw them into the pan after dredging them in flour.

In a second pan, she sautéed Brussel sprouts with fettuccine, pine nuts and onions. While the food was cooking, she went down to the basement. In the far corner was a wrought iron wine rack. She scanned the labels and pulled out a nice white Zinfandel to complement the chicken and fettuccine. CC carried her plate and glass of wine to the dining room table. She set another plate onto the floor for Bandit.

Like most of her furniture, the dining room table was 1960s Danish modern—original, not a reproduction. CC liked the straight, no-nonsense lines. It was like her—practical and efficient. After finishing dinner and her second glass of wine, she went to her desk and turned on her 23-inch iMac.

She began writing her weekly blog, called "From the Estate." It chronicled her and Anne's experiences at various sales—from estate to garage to barn. She found it a refreshing change from writing about the cold world of stainless steel, rebar and alloys.

CC used to think herself above writing a blog. After all, she was a "serious" journalist, but once she'd started, she found that she really enjoyed the process of detailing her simple weekend outings. She looked forward to sharing treasure hunting experiences with her "fans."

It wasn't just about the antiques that they found but also the journey finding them—where they ate, the sights they saw and, of course, the people they met.

"Dear Friends," CC typed. "Today Anne and I attended the estate sale of Tim Whitmore."

Chapter Six

Anne drove down Green Bay Road on the way to Great-Aunt Sybil's house. Anne was the only one she would tolerate.

She passed Walker Brothers' Pancake House and saw the long line outside the door. She fought the urge to stop for some of their fresh Lingon berry pancakes. Lingon berries reminded her of her childhood, and she could taste the sticky sweetness.

She counted the carbs in her head and admitted to herself that pancakes wouldn't be a good choice for her diet. Fighting the urge, she continued on. As she drove, a whirling dervish of upscale coffee houses, exotic car dealerships and middle-aged bottle blonde women wearing crisp white tennis skirts flew past her, making her a little dizzy. All these North Shore towns and the people who lived in them shared the same pretentious façade.

Arriving at the five-way intersection in downtown Glencoe, she struggled to remember which way to go.

Anne chose a tree-lined side street. The multi-million dollar homes were hidden behind manicured hedges. Seeing a gnome resting against a mailbox, she stopped the car. Lilac bushes that lined both sides of the long driveway were just starting to bud, releasing subtle whiffs of sweet perfume. Anne stepped out of her car, careful to avoid hitting the concrete lion on the edge of the driveway. The lawn was overgrown and weeds were sprouting everywhere. A spiny sow thistle twisted its way through a rusty wagon that Anne had played with as a child. The planters inside the wagon were bare. It wasn't like Sybil to excuse an empty flower pot. Sybil just probably never had had a chance to fill them. An early spring breeze lofting off Lake Michigan spun the wooden windmill, making a slow clacking noise like a reluctant clog dancer. Anne felt uneasy as she climbed up the front stairs of the hundred-year-old farmhouse. Two white wicker Victorian rocking chairs furnished the long, welcoming porch. Anne remembered sitting here on rainy days listening to Sybil tell tales of the North Woods while sipping Swedish Soderblandining tea. She stepped carefully as one of the floor boards sagged beneath her weight. The railing was loose, and it wobbled. This was not the house that Sybil had kept.

The leaded glass window on the chestnut door was boarded over with a piece of plywood. Even though the police had finished with the house, Anne couldn't bring herself to go inside. She sat down on one of the wicker rockers and waited for her cousin Suzanne.

Anne heard the squeal of car tires and a moment later, Suzanne was running up the walkway. "Sorry, I'm late," Suzanne said breathlessly. She was wearing dark sunglasses and a Minnesota Twins baseball cap.

Not the typical way that Anne remembered her cousin dressing.

Anne jumped up, met her cousin halfway down the stairs and gave her a big hug. "Thanks so much for coming. I really didn't want to go back inside by myself."

"I understand. I still can't believe you found her like that," Suzanne said. "Have the police found out anything?"

"There's been no update. I've been calling them. No one's gotten back to me."

"This is such a good, safe neighborhood. You don't expect anything like this to happen on the North Shore," Suzanne said.

Anne didn't answer.

Arm in arm, they walked into the house, cautiously stepping over the broken glass. "I'll get a broom," Suzanne said, walking toward the kitchen.

The Majolica umbrella stand lay on its side. Anne placed it upright, checking its rim to make sure it hadn't chipped. Its cobalt blue glaze appeared intact as were the yellow water lilies decorating its rim. She returned the collection of gold-handled walking sticks.

After cleaning the living and entry rooms, they went into Sybil's office where they encountered piles and piles of papers. Anne and Suzanne sorted through them, separating them into bills, old financial records and personal papers. Amidst the papers were scrapbooks and family photos, which they put into a large cardboard box.

The whole time they were looking at the papers, Suzanne kept her sunglasses on. "What's with the sunglasses?" Anne asked.

"I'm looking at doing Lasik and I had some testing. My eyes are sensitive to light because of the drops," Suzanne replied.

Anne shrugged it off and continued.

"I don't think we're going to finish the house today." Suzanne stood in the center of the room, holding empty cardboard banker boxes.

"I appreciate your helping me," Anne said, squatting down to fill the boxes. "I need to get all this done before the estate sale. I didn't want to be alone in the house."

Suzanne shivered and set a box down next to Anne. "It does feel creepy, doesn't it?"

Anne nodded. "Jack doesn't mind watching the kids?"

"He doesn't have the kids. They're with his parents." Suzanne sat down next to Anne. "Jack dropped me here and then went to meet some old friends at a bar in Chicago."

"Really?" Anne asked, sorting through a handful of papers and uncovering a stack of old black and white photos. "Look at all these pictures," Anne said.

"The pictures are nice, but I don't understand why she's leaving all her valuables to the Field Museum," Suzanne said.

Sybil had been a long-time patron of the Field Museum, sponsoring many exhibits. Her collection of Viking swords and jewelry were now part of its permanent collection. She had left the family memorabilia, which was priceless in both monetary and sentimental value.

"Obviously she felt they would benefit the most. Let's face it: none of us have really been around in a while," Anne said.

"She was kind of hard to be around. She wasn't really nice the past few years," Suzanne replied.

"I lived closer to her than any of the rest of the family, and I rarely made it up here. I was busy with my life and I forgot about hers."

Under a stack of papers, Anne found the family bible encased in reindeer skin. Inside it was the history of the Hillstrom family. Her eyes watered as she thought about the day not long ago when she came to the house for this bible and found Great-Aunt Sybil dead.

Anne held the wedding photo of Grandpa Booty and Grandma Lillian Hillstrom, Sybil's parents. Stan Hillstrom, or "Booty" as everyone knew him because he always wore heavy work boots, was the first of the Hillstroms to come to America. He worked as a bricklayer, saving his money to bring his wife and seven daughters to America.

Sybil often spoke of her father while she and Anne sat on her front porch. To Anne, he was a mythical figure, a new age Viking. She loved hearing stories about him. She held his picture, waiting for it to come alive, waiting for one of his smiling eyes to wink back at her.

"I don't think Sybil was in her right mind. She had gotten really forgetful, and Jack thinks she was crazy." Suzanne paused. "And a lot of the family think we should talk to an attorney about contesting the will."

"Like who?"

"Everyone. They've been calling us."

"No one's called me." Anne put the photo of Booty down. "How is Jack anyway? Has he found work yet?" Sybil wasn't the only one who hadn't liked Jack. He was a Jack-of-all-trades, master of none. Anne had hired him to do some handyman work around her bungalow. He'd charged her by the day and got very little done after his two-hour liquid lunches. His workmanship was worse than sloppy; it was criminal. Anne had to have everything he fixed, refixed after Suzanne and Jack moved to Minnesota to live with Jack's parents.

"Jack is fine. He's doing odd jobs here and there. With the economy the way it is, people can't afford custom renovations," Suzanne said.

Lucky for them, Anne thought to herself. "And the kids?" she asked.

"Kids are fine. They're in school," Suzanne said. "Jack and I were talking on the way here. You know we've been at his parent's house for a couple years now. We'd love to move back to Chicago. I could spend more time with you, and there are more opportunities for Jack here. We were thinking since the house is paid for, maybe we could make an offer to the family instead of selling it through an agent."

"How much were you thinking?" Anne asked.

"Whatever the family thought would be fair. We'd subtract our inheritance portion."

Anne breathed deeply and sighed. Family or no family—she had to ensure that Sybil's wishes were honored. "There is no inheritance. Everything is going to the Field Museum."

"If we can work things out with the attorney, maybe Jack and I could get the house and the rest of the family could split the furniture and antiques. Of course, we'd want to make some kind of donation to the Field Museum. But to just give away our family inheritance is crazy," Suzanne said.

Anne put the pictures carefully into the moving box, not wanting to respond to Suzanne. She counted to ten in her head. She turned to Suzanne. "Are you going to want any of these photos?"

"Gosh, no, you can have them all." Suzanne waved her off.

A horn blasted from the end of the driveway. Suzanne jumped up off the floor. "That must be Jack. We're staying at the Motel 6 in Evanston if you need to reach me." She hugged Anne. "Listen, Anne, I know you were closer to Sybil than the rest of us but I think the fair thing to do is to split everything up among the cousins." The horn blasted again. Suzanne glanced nervously toward the sound. "I've got to go. Jack doesn't like to wait. We'll see you tonight at Aunt Sharon's party."

Anne kissed her cousin goodbye and watched Suzanne run out the door and down the path to the waiting Jack in the gray Dodge Ram. As the couple drove off, Anne wondered if that's why Suzanne was wearing sunglasses, because Jack didn't like to wait.

Anne went back into the house to finish sorting through Sybil's massive paper files. She was covered in dust and cobwebs. Sybil had always been particular about keeping her house in perfect condition. Everyone took their shoes off at the front door, coasters under every drink. Maybe Suzanne was right. Maybe Sybil had gotten worse since Anne had seen her last. Either way, it didn't matter now. Anne went to the car and got a bucket, cleaning supplies, rubber gloves and a mop. She wanted to ready the house for the estate sale. Even more so, she didn't want any of the relatives seeing it in this condition.

A silver Bentley pulled into the driveway. Anne saw Mr. Ripley get out. "Miss Hillstrom," he said, walking up to her. He took both her hands in his. "Once again, I'm so sorry about your aunt, and I'm sorry I missed her service. I was on a buying trip that couldn't be rescheduled."

Noticing his elegant appearance, Anne looked down at her grimy clothes and wiped the cobwebs off her hair and some of the dirt smudged on her nose. "Thank you. The flowers you sent were beautiful," she said. "Thanks for meeting me here. Please come in."

Mr. Ripley followed Anne over the threshold. "You don't have to clean. My crew will handle that when they prepare the house for the sale."

"I wanted to sort through her private papers and family photos to make sure they stay in the family," Anne said, setting the bucket down in the hall.

"Of course, Anne. Any items you don't want to be sold, we will mark NFS. Make sure you tell me before the sale." Mr. Ripley looked around. Anne had removed the broken glass and tattered remains that the burglars had left behind. There were still many good antiques left.

Mr. Ripley studied the series of James Tissot framed catalog paintings hanging in the living room. Not as well known as Monet or Degas, Tissot had made a living illustrating women's clothing catalogs in the late 1800s. "The burglars must not have known the value of these Tissots. We'll get you a very good price on those," he said.

Anne stared over his shoulder, admiring the way the impressionist had captured the fashions of the Victorian ladies. His skill was evident in the way he depicted his models in their tableaux. It would be a shame to part with them. "I was actually thinking of maybe keeping those," she said.

Mr. Ripley turned and smiled at her. He strolled into the parlor and sat at the grand Steinway that filled the space. He played a Schubert piece, its lilting sound resounding throughout the room. "Your great-aunt loved Schubert," he said over his shoulder just a whisper louder than the beautiful chiming of the ancient piano.

Once again, Anne wondered if she could fit the piano into her house but the math escaped her. She might have to settle for the paintings.

Mr. Ripley stopped playing and turned around on the bench to face Anne. "I found this piano for your aunt in a small village in France called Saint-Anton-Noble-Val. I was on holiday there, sitting at an outdoor café having a delicious beef bourguignon. I heard this ethereal music drifting over the hill into the town. I followed the music to this small chateau. The man playing was a music teacher from Paris. He was living out his retirement in his family home where the piano had been for over a hundred years. He welcomed me in, and I sat and listened to him play until the sun came up. I had to have the piano. He saw how much it meant to me and being the good heart he was, he couldn't refuse me. Playing it again brings back such wonderful memories."

Listening intently, Anne felt herself sitting in that café and enjoying her crêpes. "Mmm, crêpes."

Mr. Ripley stood up. He cupped his hands behind his back as he strolled around the house, examining various items. He gave her his most charming smile and filled her ears with stories of how he came to find the items for Sybil. An old English pitcher, an Italian tapestry, a Spanish paella dish. Anne longed to accompany him on a buying trip.

When they were back in the entryway, Mr. Ripley paused and nodded. "I think this shall be a very good sale. We'll make sure each piece is given a good home. Your aunt would have wanted it that way," he said. "The Viking swords and jewelry will bring the most money. I have some buyers in mind already. I didn't see them today. I trust you have them put away for safekeeping."

"You know they're on loan to the Field Museum," Anne said.

"I was surprised that your aunt would have let them out of her sight. They are beautiful family pieces worth a fortune."

"I talked to her attorney and according to her will, she's leaving them to the Field Museum for their permanent collection."

Mr. Ripley's charming smile vanished. "This is very bad news. I'm upset for you. You could have made a lot of money from those. What about the brooch? That's the star of the collection."

"Sybil requested that it be buried with her."

Mr. Ripley's vanished smile was really gone now and not coming back. The two stood for a moment in silence. "We will make do with what we have," he said with a polished European air. "I will contact you with the final date. Is it OK if my team comes in this week to start cataloging?"

"Of course," Anne said, handing him a spare set of keys.

Mr. Ripley took Anne's hand in his. He gave her his most charming smile and said, "I'll be in touch."

Anne closed the door behind him to finish her cleaning.

Chapter Seven

Anne was running late as always. It was something she meant to work on. CC was constantly reprimanding her about her time management skills. Yes, she had many issues or as CC called them *Anne-syncrasies.* Nevertheless, she was looking forward to seeing Aunt Sharon and Uncle Dick. It was their fortieth wedding anniversary. She wished that Sybil could have been there. Sybil always liked parties, even family parties.

Anne pulled up into the driveway at Allgauer's in the Northbrook Hilton and waited for the valet. Two cars in front of her was the gray Dodge pickup. Through the back window, she could see Suzanne and Jack arguing. They were facing each other, waving their animated hands like a silent puppet show. Anne wasn't surprised to see them fighting again. Jack jumped out of the truck, slamming the door behind him. Suzanne sat with her face in her hands, her shoulders shaking like she was sobbing. Anne wanted to go over and console Suzanne but she didn't want to embarrass her. Over the past ten years, Suzanne had changed. All the life seemed to have gone out of her. Life had beaten her down, and, Anne was afraid, life wasn't the only one doing the beating.

Anne waited until Suzanne went inside and then got out of the car, handing her keys to the valet. She'd lost another two pounds on her low-carb diet and she was feeling good about the way she looked. She was wearing her brand-new purple satin dress with her vintage amethyst brooch.

All the Hillstroms were clustered at the bar. *Not too surprising,* Anne thought. Nodding at a few relatives, she walked to the bar and ordered a diet coke with lemon. She watched as Suzanne came out of the ladies' room, dabbing her eyes with a tissue. She saw Anne and put a smile on her face. Suzanne came over and sat down on the bar stool next to Anne.

"This is the most Hillstroms I've seen in one place since my wedding," Suzanne said.

"Yes. An open bar at both events." Anne raised her glass of Coke. Down the bar, an already drunk Hillstrom lifted his glass back, shouting, "Skol." Other relatives echoed his toast, raising their glasses.

Suzanne's husband, Jack, sat by himself at a table with a half-empty bottle of Absolut. *Wearing a Minnesota Vikings jersey,* Anne thought he was dressed inappropriately for such an important occasion. In contrast, Suzanne was dressed elegantly in a black silk dress with matching heels and Aunt Sybil's rhinestone jewelry. Sybil had bestowed it on Suzanne for her wedding.

The Hillstrom clan filed into the banquet hall, which was stuffed with twelve tables, each with ten chairs. Large red and yellow parrot tulips held the center at each table along with a forty-year-old wedding picture of Dick and Sharon Hillstrom. An accordion player, or as most Hillstroms called him, "Uncle Ernie," strolled from table to table, playing Swedish folk songs.

Speaking loudly over the accordion music, Anne said to Suzanne, "After you left, I found something I think that Sybil would want you to have for the kids. I have it out in my car. Maybe after the party, you can take it." As she spoke, Anne put her hand on Suzanne's forearm.

Suzanne quickly retracted it with a wince.

"What's wrong?" Anne asked.

"Nothing, just my carpal tunnel has been acting up."
For the first time, Anne noticed a wrist brace peeking out from under Suzanne's cardigan. "I'm so sorry. I've heard that's really painful."

The microphone squealed. Uncle Dick tapped on it. "Hello. Is this working? Hello? I want to thank everyone for coming out for our anniversary party. Some of you were at the wedding forty years ago and some of you weren't."

It was apparent to Anne that Uncle Dick had imbibed a little too freely. "Before we start the party, I want to raise a glass to my beautiful bride." Aunt Sharon stood next to Uncle Dick. He put his arm around her waist. They looked like a couple of Hummels, round with rosy noses and cheeks. "Here's to our first forty years together; may the next forty be as full of love and adventure. Skol!" He raised his glass.

The whole room echoed, "Skol!" And then they attacked the family smorgasbord, heaped with Swedish meatballs, potato dumplings and pickled herring. A carving station held trays of roast beef and turkey. The dancing, the feasting and the drinking continued long into the night. Sharon and Dick danced to their wedding song, "When I Fall in Love." As they were dancing, Uncle Dick grabbed the microphone and sang along with Nat King Cole, half in English and half in Swedish.

Anne and Suzanne wandered out to the car so Anne could give her the rocking horse she'd found. The bright red horse had been ridden hard by generations of Hillstroms. "I remember that rocking horse," Suzanne said. "We had to be, what? Four? Or five?"

Anne just smiled.

"The kids will. . ."

"There you are," Jack interrupted them. "Let's go." He grabbed Suzanne's arm. She moaned.

"Listen," Anne said to him, "I don't think you're in any shape to drive. I haven't been drinking. I'd be glad to drive you two back to your hotel." She stepped in between them.

Jack laughed and guzzled out of the bottle in his hand. "I'm fine to drive," he slurred his words. He grabbed Suzanne's arm again, intentionally knowing it would hurt. Suzanne pulled away and stood by Anne. Jack put the bottle down this time. "So that's how it is, is it? You know she's the one causing all the problems, Suzanne. Your cousin there. She wants to keep all the old lady's money for herself, doesn't she?"

"Jack, stop it. You're drunk. You don't know what you're saying," Suzanne said.

"The hell I don't. That old lady owed me. I fixed her porch and she never paid me."

"When did you fix her porch?" Anne asked.

"We're going now." He grabbed Suzanne, who was clutching the rocking horse. Jack grabbed the horse and smashed it to the ground. He pulled Suzanne toward their pickup.

Anne was terrified when she saw Suzanne turn around and look over her shoulder. Her eyes were empty. Whatever fight she'd once had in her was long gone.

Chapter Eight

Anne and CC arrived early at Sybil's house. Mr. Ripley was just pushing the yellow estate sale sign into the lawn. "Good morning, ladies," he nodded at them.

"We came to help," Anne said as they got out of the car. CC was carrying a cooler with sandwiches and drinks prepared for a long day and carrying the Rolleiflex 3.5F.

Mr. Ripley stopped her to admire the camera. "An early 1950s Rolleiflex. That's quite a nice camera. Where'd you find that?"

"Actually, it was at one of your sales. The Whitmore sale," CC said.

"Very nice." Mr. Ripley handed it back to CC with a smile.

"Do you need us to help set up anywhere?" Anne asked him.

"No, my staff has everything under control," Mr. Ripley said.

"We'll just look around then," Anne said.

"Is Suzanne coming later?" CC asked Anne as they walked into the house.

"She called me last night. They went back to Minnesota. She said something about one of the girls being sick," Anne said.

"That's too bad. I was looking forward to seeing her again. How are things with her and Jack?" CC asked, already knowing the answer.

"I think they've gotten worse. Jack's drinking is out of control and I know he's been taking it out on Suzanne. And there's something else, CC."

CC stared at her.

"Jack did some work on Aunt Sybil's house a couple weeks before she was murdered."

"What are you trying to say?"

"I'm not saying anything. Sybil never liked or trusted Jack. I'm sure she let Jack do the work to help Suzanne. Wait!" Anne called out to one of the workers who was setting up a table with her aunt's collection of Russian nesting dolls. The young employee halted in his tracks. "I was planning on keeping that one." Anne grabbed the four-piece set depicting the "Snow Queen" fairy tale.

CC followed in Anne's tracks, holding the items that Anne was gathering from the various rooms. "Anne, I thought you went through the house already."

"I couldn't see everything. There was so much scattered around." Anne walked over to a 1928 Max LeVerrier life-size statue light. The nude female holding a round illuminated ball symbolized the goddess of light. "NFS!" she called out urgently.

CC walked over. "Is this an original Clarte?"

"Yes, this was here when I was a child. Sybil spent a month in Europe and brought it home with her. It's a beautiful representation of art deco, isn't it?" Anne looked around. "NFS, right now, NFS!"

CC saw that Anne was losing control. She was breathing heavily, a sure sign that she would start hyperventilating at any minute. CC took her by the hand and dragged her into the bathroom which had its original white subway tile and porcelain lion-pawed bathtub.

A quick glance around and CC understood Anne's frustration. Sybil had so many beautiful antiques. It was hard to give any of them up—especially for Anne. "You can't keep everything," CC said. "Take a deep breath."

Anne took deep breaths. "CC, look, I can get another storage unit. They're not that much. I can make it work. Maybe two units."

CC smiled and gave her friend a hug. Over her shoulder, Anne caught the glint of an original Tiffany tulip vase. "NFS!" she called out. "NFS, NFS!" She pointed at the vase. CC saw a wild look in Anne's eyes, like she'd jumped into the abyss. "Take a breath, Anne; we'll work all this out, I promise."

Anne just shut her eyes and repeated, "NFS, NFS," her new mantra. A tap on the door broke Anne's meditation. "Ladies, is everything okay?" Mr. Ripley asked through the closed door.

"Yes, Mr. Ripley, we'll be right out. Everything's fine," replied CC.

The bathroom door opened and the two women emerged, just as the front door swung open and people started filing into the house. Sipping her coffee, CC settled herself at a perch in the kitchen. Anne wandered behind customers, trying to talk them out of items, showcasing flaws and mismarkings with a gleeful enthusiasm. CC shook her head. For the most part, CC was proud of her friend. She had the key to the candy store, but she wasn't eating all the candy.

After many hours, the sale was winding down. CC thought Anne would make it, until Betsy Buttersworth walked in. CC had hoped, no, she'd prayed, that Buttersworth didn't know about the sale. When she hadn't seen Betsy first thing in the morning, she'd thought they had been lucky. It turned out they were not so lucky.

Mr. Ripley hurried over to greet Betsy, one of his best customers. He did his European hand kiss that he apparently reserved for very special clients, CC thought. Betsy had brought her entourage, or as she referred to them, "the ladies." Supposedly they were a book club, but there was little reading involved.

Anne had not seen them yet. She was arguing with a customer over a Lalique vase in the sitting room. All of a sudden, the vase crashed to the floor when Anne spotted Buttersworth. All eyes turned to look at Anne. CC could see the letters "NFS" forming on Anne's lips but it was too late. Betsy was holding the silver Tiffany pine-needle-pattern letter holder and its accompanying inkwell.

Betsy handed it to one of Mr. Ripley's assistants and continued onto the Majolica umbrella stand. "This would be perfect in the lake house," she chortled to her gang.

The Betsy clones all nodded in unison. Anne was terrified. She'd thought she'd put a sticker on it. She ran over. "Oh, Buttersworth, thank you for coming." Anne wrapped her arms around the umbrella stand.

"Hillstrom, so sorry for your loss," Betsy said. "Your aunt had very good taste."

Anne held onto the umbrella stand with a vise-like grip. "Yes, she did. Very good taste. The NFS sticker must have fallen off the umbrella stand. I'll get another one."

"Don't bother. I've already told Mr. Ripley I'm taking it," Betsy said.

Anne was at a loss for words. She couldn't go against estate sale protocol. She released her grip, still smiling and backed away slowly. But not without removing the gold-handled canes from the umbrella stand, clutching them tightly to her chest. "These don't come with the umbrella stand."

Betsy reneged on this battle, but her onslaught continued as she walked through the house and pointed at items. Mr. Ripley's assistant stuck sold stickers on them. It was like Sherman marching through Atlanta to the sea. CC covered Anne's eyes and took her to the backyard. "You don't need to see this. Remember, all the proceeds are going to the museum. It was Sybil's wish."

"Yes, I know." Anne cleared her eyes, took a deep breath and nodded. "I'm okay. Sybil left me her most precious possessions. I've got all the family photos and the family bible. Those are really the most important things, right? Right, CC?"

"Yes, it is," CC reassured her.

Mr. Ripley showed the last customer out at 4:15 p.m. and closed the door behind him. His assistants scurried around, making notes about items that were to be shipped or picked up later. Mr. Ripley counted the receipts for the day. He motioned for Anne to come to him. "I don't have a complete tally yet, but from what we sold today and from what buyers I have lined up for the piano and larger items, I estimate about $350,000. Of course, that's after my twenty-five percent commission," he said. "And, if you'd consider letting other items go, we could potentially make closer to $500,000."

The numbers filtered through Anne's head. She wasn't concerned about the money so much, but rather preserving the precious memories. Except for Buttersworth, Anne knew in her heart that the items had gone to good, loving homes. She had interviewed each recipient carefully.

Chapter Nine

CC sat down at her computer and went to her blog site. "Dear Friends, today Anne and I attended the estate sale of Anne's Great-Aunt Sybil," she wrote. "As you may have read in my previous blog post, Sybil was killed by a burglar who ransacked her house. We thank you for all your condolences and comments. We appreciate the flowers that were sent to the wake. It was very generous. We feel that you are all part of our extended family.

"At today's sale, Anne found it difficult to part with many of her aunt's treasures. She decided to add certain pieces to her own collection." CC uploaded photos of the nesting dolls, the statue and the Tissot catalog drawings. "Anne was very careful to make sure that every item went to a good home. Thankfully, Sybil's most precious possessions—the Hillstrom heirloom Viking swords and jewelry—were already on loan to the Field Museum. As per Sybil's request, those items are now part of the museum's permanent collection. If you have the opportunity, you should go visit the museum and stop by the Hillstrom exhibit. There are some beautiful gold and precious stone bracelets and rings." CC continued to expound on Sybil's collection, occasionally reaching down to pet Bandit who was sleeping on her feet.

Before going to bed, CC checked her blog and saw one new comment. "Anne and CC, so sorry about Aunt Sybil. Our prayers are with you. I wanted to share that when I was at the Elkhorn flea market, I saw a vendor selling some Viking jewelry. I don't know enough about this kind of jewelry to say if it was real or not, but he was asking a lot of money for it. It's the first time I've seen this kind of jewelry for sale at this market. Your friend, Pam."

CC googled *Elkhorn flea market* and saw that it was open this Sunday, tomorrow. She texted Anne all the details.

Chapter Ten

It was 5 a.m., much too early to be awake on a Sunday morning. But if there was a chance to find some of Aunt Sybil's lost, stolen jewelry, it was worth sacrificing her sleep. Plus, after all, it was a flea market. Anne's life was spent searching for new places to shop. The monthly antique market opened at 7 a.m., and Elkhorn, Wisconsin, was at least a 90-minute drive so they had to get moving.

Anne waited impatiently for CC to arrive, upset that CC had to stop at Starbuck's on the way to her house. There would be plenty of time for coffee later. CC pulled up, sipping her Grande Americano. "I want to beat traffic," she called out from the open driver's window.

Traffic, Anne thought, as she settled into the passenger seat. *Who else would be crazy enough to be out at this hour?* They took the highway until it ended at Lake Cook Road and then meandered along Route 12; nothing was open and no one was on the road.

"Oh, did I tell you? CC, it was fantastic! Last weekend when I went to my Aunt Sharon's fortieth wedding anniversary, I brought along the dress I'd worn as a flower girl. My mom had it specially made from this Irish linen fabric. We hung the dress up for everyone to see, and they were so impressed with the quality."

"I like that old picture of you that you emailed to me, wearing the dress as a flower girl. It looked great," CC said, keeping her eyes on the road.

"I brought out the Hillstrom bible too. I found it when Suzanne and I were clearing out Sybil's house," Anne said.

"How is Suzanne?"

"She looked beautiful. Jack was drunk." Anne paused for a moment. "It was nice going through the family history with everyone at the party. A lot of my cousins didn't know anything about our heritage or our ancestors," Anne said. "According to some of the earlier entries, the Hillstroms date back to the ninth century Vikings."

"That's really interesting. You know, Anne, the word *Viking* originates from the Old Norse and literally translated means *expedition overseas*," CC said.

"Yes, I knew that, CC, very interesting," Anne replied, digging through her purse for a mint.

"Did I tell you? Dannie is pregnant again." CC changed the subject, talking about her stepdaughter, Dannie.

"Oooh, babies! That's so exciting. When is she due?"

"Sometime in the fall," CC replied.

They continued to exchange news during the remainder of the drive to Elkhorn. Upon arriving in the city, they made a brief pit stop at a gas station. Once back in the car and on the main street, they arrived at the entrance to the fairgrounds' parking lot where a policeman was directing traffic. They followed his directions and parked. The lot was already packed with cars and people were waiting eagerly in line by the front gate. Many were wheeling carts, wagons and baskets. Although the weatherman had predicted temperatures in the upper 80s, the morning air was cool and overcast. After they parked, Anne slathered her milky white skin with SPF 45. That and her blonde hair were gifts from her Viking ancestors.

They took their place in line, Anne waiting impatiently. "C'mon, we're all here. Why can't they just let us in?"

"Because it's not seven yet," CC said, spraying herself liberally with suntan lotion.

Anne flipped open her phone and looked at the time. "It's 6:58; close enough."

"Really?" CC asked. "You're going to start the day like this?"

The line started moving forward and finally they went through the gate. Despite the cool chill, Anne felt sticky, especially when the sun peeked through the clouds. She was excited about the possibilities of what she might find. The fairgrounds resembled a Turkish bazaar with rows of long tables, some covered by canopies, with vendors selling goods out of the back of their vans.

They walked to the first booth, Anne inspecting every piece. She'd brought her magnifying loupe for close examination. She picked up an early Limoges gravy boat. *It was $42 too much*, she thought, putting it back down.

CC wandered along, looking at industrial merchandise like old tools, beat-up storage lockers, farm implements and finally honing in on an old miniature lead airplane. She just had to have it. She bartered with the man, settling on a price. Out of the corner of her eye, she saw Anne frantically waving at her. CC walked over to where Anne was almost jumping up and down. No small feat.

"Look at this French provincial cabinet. Isn't it gorgeous? It would look fantastic in your living room," Anne said, pointing at a large gold gilt cabinet with a glass front.

CC walked all around the piece, inspecting every inch of both its exterior and its interior. "I'm not looking for any furniture," she told Anne.

"You have to have it. Look at the price. It's a bargain," Anne argued.

CC studied it. It was an extremely handsome piece. She hesitated.

"Sit down." Anne pulled her over to a nearby bench. "Just sit here and look at it," she said.

CC sat down next to her. The two sat and stared at the cabinet, admiring its curved legs, ornately painted front and the overall craftsmanship. "Try to convince me that you can live without it," Anne said. Anne had a way of wearing CC's resistance down. It's not that CC didn't appreciate the piece and that she didn't want it. She just didn't need it. Her German sensibility often kept her from making impulse decisions, whereas Anne lived by them.

"I do like it, and it would look nice in my living room," CC said.

The old grizzly-haired gentleman who ran the booth walked over to them. "What do you think? I've seen you staring at this cabinet? It's a great cabinet. I can make you a great deal."

"Problem is, I have no way of getting it back to my house," CC said, touching the cabinet with her fingers.

"For a small fee, I can deliver it for you," he said.

"We'll take it," Anne exclaimed, jumping up.

They settled on a price, exchanged information and then went on to the next booth. Anne stopped to admire an early 20th century oak fireplace mantel. It was just what she'd been looking for to replace the one in her living room. Even though she hadn't measured the space, she just knew it would fit.

While transfixed by the fireplace mantel, she saw a lady pick up a Roseville magnolia vase. *It was priced way too high,* she thought. "That's not real," she whispered over the lady's shoulder.

The woman turned and looked at her, "How do you know?"

"If it was a real Roseville, the magnolias would be better defined. This glaze is too rough. An authentic Roseville has a slight shine to the glaze and the detail is more precisely painted. Turn it over and look at the lettering. On a real Roseville the *s* will slant slightly to the right; see this one is straight up and down," Anne said, pleased with herself for passing along valuable information. She always liked to share her knowledge with a fellow enthusiast.

"Thank you," the woman said, putting the vase back down and walking away.

While Anne was pondering various items, CC spotted a bright blue decorated ceramic tile in a neighboring booth. She wandered over to take a closer look. "Pewabic pottery, $35," she read. She got excited. Founded in Detroit in 1903, Pewabic pottery was very collectible and growing in value. If this was authentic, she could make a profit right here, right now, reselling it on eBay.

She pulled out her iPhone and went to the eBay app. Similar tiles were selling for hundreds. Pulling out her reading glasses, she turned the tile onto its back so she could take a closer look at the mark. The copyright mark was 1997. She put it back disappointed. Earlier work by the company was highly sought after; the more recent pieces, while still collectible, were not as valuable.

CC continued to the next booth in search of a find.

Anne continued her hunt, picking up a little trinket here and there, a depression glass bottle stopper, a hand-woven towel, a postcard of Erte art and the *piece de resistance*—a small pair of scissors in the shape of an ostrich. Somehow, she'd misplaced CC. She scanned the growing crowd but could not see her friend. She did smell popcorn, however. Maybe it was time for a snack. While paying for her popcorn, CC walked over to her, carrying a large pine spice box. "Isn't this awesome?" she asked.

"That's fantastic," Anne replied, a mouth full of kettle corn.

"I'm going to use it for my art supplies," CC said, admiring the clean lines of the box.

"Are you ready to go? I'm so hot," Anne said.

"Aren't you enjoying yourself?" CC asked, stopping to peruse a display of watch parts. "I think we've been to every booth, and I haven't seen anything that even resembles Viking jewelry."

Out of the corner of her eye, Anne glimpsed some jewelry display cases lined up on a table in front of a white panel van. "CC, one quick look before we go." Munching on her popcorn, she strolled over to the table. It was a mishmash of vintage jewelry with some cheap Avon pieces and some slightly better silver tossed in.

"Do you see anything you like? I can work with you," the man from behind the table said, getting up from his lawn chair.

"That's okay," Anne said, turning away.

"Wait; I just got some new stuff in." The man went into the van and pulled out a shoebox. He set it down on the table in front of Anne who out of politeness picked through the rings and bracelets. Most were silver or brass. She came across a gold band which stood out from amongst the rest. Anne held it up to admire it in the sunlight.

"You have a good eye. That's a really good piece. It's solid gold," he said.

Anne pulled her jeweler's loupe out of her large orange Prada bag to examine the crudely hammered metal. She peered closely inside the band and noticed what looked like the Hillstrom crest. This could be one of the Hillstrom Viking rings that had been passed down to Sybil; Anne was sure of it. "This looks really old. Where did you get this?"

"I buy from a lot of different dealers in Chicago."

"This particular ring. Where'd you get this one?"

He stammered, "I don't remember exactly." His eyes shifted around the perimeter. He took the ring back and put it away. "If you're not going to buy something, I need you to make room for other people."

"I'm interested. How much do you want?" Anne pulled the ring back from the box.

"I think the gold alone is worth $300," he said.

Anne reached into her purse and pulled out three one hundred dollar bills. "I'll give you two hundred for the ring and a hundred more if you tell me where you got it. I collect old rings, and I'd really like to see more of this type."

"I get a lot of gold bands. I believe this one came from a pawnshop at Western and Division in Chicago. It's called Metro Sales." He scratched his head.

Anne handed him the money and slipped the ring into her purse. "Now, I'm ready to go," Anne said, turning back to CC who had watched the whole scene in disbelief.

"I'm surprised you didn't try to talk him down," CC said as they walked out the flea market entrance.

Anne's feet were sore after walking around the flea market for four and a half hours. It was now 11:30 a.m. and the sun was heating up. *It must be at least 90 degrees,* she thought. She could feel the sun hitting the back of her neck and was glad to be heading home. Maybe she could take an afternoon nap or run to Goodwill. She'd have to wait until Monday to visit the pawn store.

Chapter Eleven

After dropping Anne off, CC headed home. She walked Bandit around the block. The dog wasn't really good in the heat but needed the exercise. When they came back, she poured herself a glass of wine and sat in front of her computer. She uploaded the pictures she'd taken at the flea market from her iPhone.

She started typing, "Dear Friends, Anne and I had a pretty successful day at the Wisconsin flea market. It was our first time venturing north. It was a mixture of some very nice antiques, but a lot of junk. Like with everything, you have to pick and choose. I've posted some pictures of some of the items we found. We had a delightful lunch at a little pancake house along Route 12. I also posted pictures of the omelet I had with a side of homemade blueberry pancakes. Yum Yum. Anne was very helpful with helping me find this lovely French provincial cabinet for my living room. She also saved a woman from buying a fake Roseville vase. Once again, it's very important to know what you're buying before you buy it." CC sat back, gulped her wine and pondered the day's events. She then went back to typing, "The important thing as always is not so much what I found as who I found it with. The best find is an old friend."

As she stopped for another sip of wine, she noticed a comment from a reader. "Dear Friend, my name is Ida. I live in New Buffalo, Michigan. One of my girlfriends from Bingo told me about your blog, and I'm so glad she did. I've really enjoyed reading about you and Anne and your adventures. I feel like I know you both. Because of you, I was inspired to buy something that I've always wanted. When I was a little girl, my mother gave me a Steiff bear. We didn't have a lot of money, and they really couldn't afford it. It meant so much for her to give it to me. Somewhere over the fifty years that passed, I lost that bear. My daughter is having my first grandchild now. As you might imagine, we are all very excited and I feel very blessed. I wanted to have a special gift for her, so I bought an antique Steiff bear that looks similar to the one I had when I was a little girl. It cost me most of my savings but it's worth every penny to pass this tradition on to my grandchild. I've attached a picture of it. I wanted to thank you so much for inspiring me. Your friend, Ida from New Buffalo, Michigan."

CC opened the picture. It appeared to be a vintage Steiff bear in very good condition; however, there were some signs that had her questioning its authenticity. She zoomed in on the picture, but couldn't see clearly enough to tell if her suspicions were correct. It made her feel bad for Ida and angry at whoever'd deceived her.

She quickly clicked *reply* and typed, "Dear Ida, Thank you so much for the lovely message. You seem like a wonderful woman, and I'm very happy that you are able to pass this tradition to your grandchild. I would love to meet you in person and see the bear. Please let me know if I can pay you a visit. Your friend, CC."

Chapter Twelve

Anne ducked out of work early. She wanted to get to the pawnshop before rush hour. The intersection at Western and Division was lined with currency exchanges, Laundromats, taco stands and several pawnshops. It was a neighborhood transitioning from low-income housing to upscale condo development. *Still best to travel there during daylight hours*, Anne thought, looking for the sign that said Metro Sales.

She found it on a dingy storefront with blacked out windows. Iron bars encased the windows and the front door. She circled the block several times, looking for a parking space and finally found one a half block down. Clutching her purse closely, she scurried down the sidewalk, avoiding eye contact. As she stepped off the curb to cross the alleyway, a homeless man in tattered jeans with a toothless smile jumped in front of her. Anne gasped and stopped in her tracks.

"Excuse me, ma'am. Can you help me out? You see my shoes." He glanced at his feet. Anne gazed down to see his torn and tattered gym shoes. "I just got out of the 51st station jail and I could use some help with some shoes."

His sincerity surprised her. From the smell of alcohol on his breath, she'd expected him to ask for the money for something else. She moved her purse in front of her and dug into her jeans, pulling out a five-dollar bill. She handed it to him. "God bless you," he said, stepping out of her way.

Anne hurried past him and the three remaining storefronts. She rang the buzzer to enter the pawnshop, keeping watch around her. The buzzer sounded and she pushed open the heavy door. Inside, was a small narrow aisle with glass display cases on each side, overflowing with broken dreams.

Behind the bulletproof glass, sat a large man sitting on a much too small metal stool, with an unlit cigar dangling from his mouth. His dark eyes twinkled under the furry caterpillar that crawled across his brow. His head was free of hair. His thick black moustache danced as he spoke. "Can I help you?"

Anne dug into her large orange Prada bag and retrieved the gold band. She placed it in the exchange slot under the glass. "Can you tell me about this ring?"

He picked it up and examined it closely with his loupe. "It's a very old ring." He paused and nodded. "I remember this now. It's a Viking wedding band from about 800 AD. I sold it to Marvin, another dealer."

"Yes, I know. I bought it from him at the flea market," Anne said impatiently. "I want to know where you got it."

"Why do you need to know that?"

"I collect Viking jewelry," Anne said. "Do you have any more pieces like this?"

"No." He shook his head and put the ring back under the glass exchange slot.

Anne grabbed the ring and slid it back in her purse. "How about the person you got this from? Do they have more?"

"I don't recall off the top of my head."

"You must have a record of the sale."

He chewed his cigar and ran his hand over his smooth scalp. The metal chair creaked as he shifted his weight. "Look, lady, I get a lot of people in here. I don't need to know their stories. I don't have any Viking jewelry. Do you want to see something else?"

"Thank you, you've been helpful." She turned and walked out of the store. She rushed back to her car and clicked the locks. She found the nearest police station on the map app on her phone and drove to it. Walking to the front desk, she said to the sergeant on duty, "My name is Anne Hillstrom. I'd like to see a detective."

"What's it about?" he asked.

"It's about stolen property," she said.

"Have a seat," he said, pointing to a line of wooden benches against the wall. "I'll call someone down."

A short while later, a very tall, thin man stood before Anne. "Miss Hillstrom," he said. "I'm Detective Towers." At six foot seven, his name was appropriate. He hunched over to speak with her eye-to-eye. Anne thought he resembled a question mark. She was surprised to hear the British accent coming out of a Chicago police detective. He didn't look anything like a Chicago cop. His sunflower tie seemed out of place for such a serious job.

He noticed her staring at his tie. "A bit of whimsy helps put people at ease and keeps a smile on my face."

Anne smiled.

"Why don't we go to my desk? We can have a chat," Detective Towers said.

Anne followed him up the stairs. By the second flight, Anne thought, *Ok, I'm going to plug in the damn treadmill when I get home.*

Detective Towers held a chair out for Anne and then sat behind a metal desk in a large open office. The room was noisy and crowded with other detectives. "May I get you something to drink?" he asked.

"No, thank you."

"Right then. Sergeant Wilkins said something about stolen property?"

Anne pulled the ring out of her purse. "I bought this ring at a flea market in Wisconsin. When I looked inside, I saw what I thought was my family crest, the Hillstrom crest. I know it's a Viking wedding band. My aunt had a large collection of Viking jewelry." She paused. "Anyway, my aunt Sybil—actually she was my great aunt—she was killed a few weeks ago. Someone broke in and robbed her and killed her."

"I'm very sorry to hear about your Great Aunt," Detective Towers said with a genuine sincerity. "Was this one of the items taken?" He looked up from his notebook where he'd been scribbling.

"I don't know. I hadn't seen the ring before but it sure looks like the Hillstrom crest."

"Do you have a list of what was taken?"

"Not really." Anne paused. "I hadn't seen my aunt in years. None of the family had. I don't exactly know all the items that were taken. What I knew I gave to the Glencoe police."

"She lived in Glencoe?"

"Yes."

"You should speak with them if it's an ongoing investigation."

"The guy at the flea market bought it from a pawn store at Western and Division. I asked the owner there about it, and he couldn't remember where he got it. But doesn't the law require him to keep a record?"

Detective Towers stopped writing. "Miss Hillstrom, I'm sorry about your aunt. I'll call the Glencoe police, and I'll stop by the pawnshop. May I keep the ring?" he asked. "I'll write you a receipt for it."

Anne hesitated. "Is that really necessary?"

Detective Towers smiled. "I promise I'll get it back to you personally."

Chapter Thirteen

It was another early weekend morning. Anne was sitting shotgun while CC drove. They were heading across the border to visit Ida in person. Even at this time of the morning, there was bumper-to-bumper traffic at the merge of 294/94. This route headed them right through Gary, Indiana, a trip CC knew well from frequent visits to Gary Works, the Midwest outpost of US Steel. Chicagoans frowned on Gary, Indiana. It was Chicago's New Jersey. From the thick smoke bellowing out of the steel plant to the abundance of bail bondsmen along the main drag, Gary had a bad reputation as "Murder Capital of the United States."

CC was a hardened journalist. She went where the steel was. She had spent time in all the tough blue-collar towns in the Midwest—Detroit, Cleveland, and Gary. Location didn't bother her. She felt at ease in a hard hat or drinking a beer with the boys from the mill.

As they drove, she explained to Anne about the inner workings of the Gary plant. "You wouldn't believe it, Anne, it's so hot in the furnace room. The temperature from the blast reaches up to 2300 degrees. I was behind the scenes on the catwalk, but you can take a similar tour. It's open to the public. You can see them make steel for automotive and appliance manufacturers. It's very impressive," CC said. "If you want, maybe we can stop on our way back."

Anne cleared her throat and put down her tourist guide. "You know, I was just looking in this book and was hoping we could stop in Nappanee on the way back. It's not that far from New Buffalo."

"Nappanee?"

"That's where Amish Acres is. I thought we could eat dinner at the restaurant and visit the little shops. The restaurant received phenomenal reviews on Yelp. You can watch them make candles, soap and their own jam. It's the original farm to table. These Amish don't fool around," Anne said.

"Let's see how much time we have after we meet with Ida," CC said, but she knew Anne had already made up her mind.

"I meant to tell you about the ring I bought in Elkhart," Anne said. "I didn't want to say anything because I was afraid you'd think I was being dramatic. The ring was engraved with what I thought was the Hillstrom family crest."

CC cocked her head sideways to look at Anne for a clearer understanding of what she was saying. "Was it?"

"The markings are pretty worn, but I know that crest. I've seen it on other family heirlooms that Sybil had," Anne said. "I actually found out where the flea market dealer bought it from. It was a pawnshop in Chicago. I went and talked to the owner."

"Do you think it was stolen from Sybil? Is that why?"

"Of course," Anne said. "The owner wasn't very helpful so I went to the police. I talked to a detective about the ring. His name is Nigel Towers. He's British," Anne said enthusiastically.

"What do you mean he's British?"

"Originally he's from England. He lives here now, of course. And, he's really tall."

"What about the ring? What did he find out?" CC interrupted her.

"Yeah, the ring, Nigel. . ."

"Nigel?" CC interrupted again.

"Yes, Nigel; that's his name. I told you, he's going to talk to the pawnshop owner."

"I hope they find who took the ring. It may lead them to Sybil's killer," CC said.

The short ride took a long time because of the traffic and construction curving around the heel of Lake Michigan. They stopped for breakfast in New Buffalo. CC had heard from colleagues about a fantastic cafe called Nani's on Red Arrow Highway.

The parking lot was crowded. Its reputation kept the seats full. "Smells good. Let's see if we can get a table," Anne said.

After a short wait, the girls were seated at a table overlooking the highway, which was really more of a two-lane country road. The harbor area, as New Buffalo was known, was the weekend playground of Chicago's wealthier residents. It boasted lots of upscale little boutiques and bistros situated on the shores of Lake Michigan. Both Anne and CC felt at home in such a quaint town.

Looking at the menu, CC said, "This maple bacon muffin sound delish. Anything with bacon in it, I'm on board." She closed her menu decisively. CC picked up her coffee cup and cradled it in her hands, blowing away the steam.

Anne had not looked at her menu yet. She was busy admiring the local artwork that adorned the walls. It was a cozy little spot with a beachfront flavor. It was early June, and the summer crowd was just starting to arrive. The waitress brought over their food. Anne had ordered the lemon rosemary muffin and a raspberry spice tea. CC stuck with her original plan and had the maple bacon muffin.

They enjoyed their muffins in silence. Anne browsed through a local shop paper, reading occasionally aloud to CC.

CC half listened as she stared out the window. She watched a white Ford F100 pickup pull into the parking lot. It seemed out of place amidst the Range Rovers and Lexuses. She was losing interest until the driver stepped out. She recognized him almost immediately—he was the man from the train. He had lost the sports jacket and was wearing a t-shirt and was wearing it well. She reached in her purse and reapplied her lipstick.

Anne looked up, her nose above the brochure. "What are you doing?"

"My lips are dry."

Anne ignored her friend's answer, sticking her nose back in the glossy paper, trying to determine if they would have time to visit the farmer's market she'd seen advertised.

CC adjusted herself and fluffed her hair. Picking up a butter knife, she tried to catch her reflection to make sure that everything was the best it could be. It was a very good move on her part as she caught the little piece of bacon stuck between her front teeth. She suddenly wished she wasn't in her plaid Bermuda shorts and tank top. It wasn't her best look. *What am I doing?* she thought. *I don't even know this guy. It was a glance on the train. He's probably here meeting his wife or fiancé or even his boyfriend.*

The man from the train sat down at a stool at the counter. CC overheard him ordering a black coffee and a bacon maple muffin.

Okay; he's got good taste, she thought.

The waitress came over. "Anything else?"

"No, we're fine," Anne said, looking up. "Just the check."

While CC glanced over her shoulder to glimpse the man from the train, Anne figured out the bill. "Your share comes to $8, CC," Anne said.

"What? Okay," CC said, looking back at Anne. She pulled out $10 and threw it on the table. Her journalist's instinct kicked in. There was a story here, and she wanted to get to it. However, now was not the time.

As she walked out to the parking lot, she glanced into the bed of his truck. She saw woodworking tools and paintbrushes. They left Nani's, and the man from the train in the rearview mirror.

A short while later, they pulled up in front of Ida's two bedroom, white clapboard cottage. They could tell she wasn't a woman of means. Getting out of the car, CC pulled open the white picket fence that encircled the house. The sweet perfume of the old English roses floated up as she walked past them. Lined along the front steps, the potted Gerbera daisies greeted a cheerful hello. Ida waved from the front picture window. For an older woman using a walker, she made it to the front door quickly. "CC, Anne, I'm so glad you came," Ida said, opening the screen door to let them in. "You look just like your pictures. I'm Ida. Come on in." Ida walked slowly back to the living room, her arthritic hands clutching the walker.

The living room was crowded with furniture, including comfortable wingback chairs, a drum table and a curio cabinet. Family photographs in assorted frames and sizes cluttered the room from the walls to the table. Anne paused to admire the older frames particularly a large Eastlake frame. She wondered if Ida would consider selling it.

Ida picked up a photograph from the table next to her chair. It was a wedding photo of a young couple. "That's my daughter, Rose, and her husband, Marco. This was taken two years ago. She's expecting my first grandchild." Ida sank down into a worn out recliner. Next she picked up another photo—this time a black and white wedding photo. "That's my Charles. Everyone called him Charlie." She lovingly traced the frame with her index finger. "He was a school teacher. He taught history at the middle school in New Buffalo. He passed 20 years ago."

CC stood over Ida's shoulder, admiring the photos. "You and your daughter were both beautiful brides."

"Thank you," Ida said. "I made us some lemonade. Please come into the kitchen."

She led the way into a small, cozy kitchen with a round oak table. She went over to the refrigerator, struggling to lift out a pitcher while holding onto her walker.

CC walked over, grabbing the pitcher. "Let me help you with that."

"Thank you, dear." Ida sat down at the table. "There's glasses up there, dear." She pointed to a cabinet over the sink.

CC poured them all a glass of homemade lemonade. She looked out the kitchen window and saw the rose bushes in the backyard. "Your roses are beautiful."

"I'm having a difficult time this year. The flowers aren't as full as they've been. It seems like the petals are wilting before they even flower," Ida said.

"Do you have a pail?" CC asked.

"Sure, dear; there's one outside by the back door."

Standing by the sink, CC took the dish soap and went into the backyard. She filled the pail with water and soap. She walked to the roses and one by one picked the Japanese beetles off the bush, dropping them into the water. Anne and Ida stood watching CC from the kitchen window.

When CC had disposed of the unwanted intruders, she joined the two women back in the kitchen. "Ida, your problem was Japanese beetles. I didn't think they were in Michigan. We've seen a lot in Illinois the last couple years."

"Oh, my word."

"They won't kill your plants. They just eat the petals from the inside out. The best thing is to pick them off and throw them in soapy water. You can plant tansy and chives around the roses to keep them out," CC said.

"Thank you, dear. I haven't been out in the garden a lot this year. Excuse me for a moment." She walked out of the kitchen. A few minutes later, she came back carrying a teddy bear. "This is it. This is the bear I was telling you about. It looks remarkably similar to the one I had as a child in the 1950s." She handed the bear to CC who carefully looked it over. CC gave it to Anne who examined it closely. CC and Anne looked at each other. They were in agreement.

"Ida, I noticed from the pictures you sent me of the bear," CC said, "that something might not be quite right. I didn't want to say anything until I could see the bear in person to see its serial number. You can see that the ear is missing the button that Steiff bears should have. This bear's serial number ends with 22. The last number represents the centimeter of the bear. This bear is much smaller than 22 centimeters. Somebody tried hard to pass this off as an authentic Steiff bear. I'm sorry to say, Ida, it's not."

Ida started to cry. Anne put her arm around her. "I'm such a foolish woman. The man at the store seemed so nice. He assured me this bear was real. He said it was the same year as my original childhood bear. I paid him $1,200. That was everything I had."

Anne reached into her purse and pulled out a lacy monogrammed handkerchief. She handed it to Ida.

"Ida, Anne and I will take the bear and go talk to the shop owner. Maybe he made a mistake," CC said.

Ida looked up. "You would do that for me?"

"Of course, we will." Anne said.

Chapter Fourteen

Talcott's Collectibles resembled a junkyard more than an antique store. Tires, out-of-season snow shovels were haphazardly displayed next to cheap ceramic planters. Other shelves bore bargain basement seasonal items like swimming goggles, water pistols and mittens. Even Anne was hard pressed to find anything she would consider picking up.

Mr. Talcott greeted them at the counter. He was a gruff older gentleman wearing a not so clean tank top, khaki pants and sandals. "Can I help you, ladies?" he asked, pushing his glasses down his nose to get a better view.

CC held the bear up. "Yes, you can. My friend bought this bear from you and apparently she thought it was a genuine Steiff bear. It's obviously not."

Mr. Talcott took the bear out of her hands and gave it a quick uninterested once over, handing it back to Anne. "Do you have a receipt?"

"No, I don't. My friend, Ida, seemed to misplace it."

"Sorry, I can't do anything for you without a receipt. How do I know she bought it here?"

Anne walked up behind CC with a handful of similar fake Steiff bears. "Sure looks similar to these. You have a whole shelf of them."

"Look, ladies, everything here is sold as is. Without a receipt, I can't help you. If you're not going to buy something, I need you to leave."

Anne put the bears on the counter and was about to go into action. CC grabbed her elbow and said, " Thank you." She started to pull Anne out of the store. Anne reached over her shoulder and grabbed Ida's bear back.

"What are you doing? This guy obviously is a crook," Anne complained loudly.

"There's no talking to guys like that. We're going to have to figure something else out," CC said.

Getting back in the car, they pulled up in front of the *New Buffalo Daily Star* newspaper office. CC led the way. A young college grad greeted them from the reception desk. "How can I help?"

"My name is CC. This is Anne. Can I talk to the news editor about a story?"

"I'll get Mrs. Bradley." The intern got up and walked to an office. A few minutes later, a woman in her thirties came over to them. "Can I help you?" she asked.

CC introduced herself and Anne. "I wanted to talk to you about Talcott's Collectibles."

"That place is a real eyesore," Mrs. Bradley said. "People complain about it all the time, but there's not much we can do. The store does a good business with the seasonal crowd."

Anne held up the bear. "Did you know about this?"

"What is it?" Mrs. Bradley asked.

"It's a fake Steiff bear that he's selling. He's got a whole shelf of them."

At her blank stare, CC explained, "Steiff bears were founded in Germany in the 1800s and are still handmade today. They are highly collectible."

"That's interesting. I haven't heard anything about Talcott selling fake bears." Mrs. Bradley stared at them in curiosity. "Just who are you?"

"We're antique hunters," Anne said.

"What do you want me to do about the bears?" Mrs. Bradley prodded.

"Can you write a story to warn people? They need to know that these bears are fake before they buy them," CC said. "Unless you know what you're looking for, it's a pretty good imitation."

"Explain how you know they're fake," Mrs. Bradley said.

CC and Anne walked her through how to identify real Steiff bears from fake ones.

"Kristin, come here a minute." Mrs. Bradley motioned to the intern. "I want you to take a ride over to Talcott's and see what you can find out about these bears."

Anne and CC thanked Mrs. Bradley. They went back to Ida's house. Ida was waiting for them in the front yard. She was picking Japanese beetles off the roses. Anne handed her back the bear.

"That Mr. Talcott is not a nice man, Ida," CC said. "I'm sorry we weren't able to get your money back, but I did talk to the local paper and they're going to write a story about him. That way he can't fool other people."

"We're not going to give up on this. I promise we'll do all we can to get your money back," Anne said.

Ida hugged both girls and gave them a homemade loaf of banana bread. The girls headed back to the highway.

"I don't know about you but I'm starving and Nappanee is only 30 minutes away. Thresher's restaurant is supposed to have a fantastic chicken dinner."

Nappanee was home to Amish Acres, the 138-year-old homestead of Indiana's Amish population. Popular with tourists, the homestead had been restored to a living history museum. It offered tours, musical theater and, of course, old-fashioned family-style dinners. CC and Anne had often talked about visiting, but had never found time until now. They arrived just in time for the dinner rush, put their names in and wandered around the little stores by the restaurant.

Anne examined the handcrafted knives, tasted the fresh-made jam and smelled the beeswax candles. She touched all the quilts as she tried to pick out her favorite pattern. CC sat reading a book on Amish life. When their names were called for dinner, they sat at the old-fashioned barn table. The waitress dressed in an ankle-length black dress with a white apron and white bonnet, greeted them.

The biscuits arrived first, still warm. Anne smothered hers with the freshly churned butter. Then came the broasted chicken and honey-glazed ham with mashed potatoes.

CC reached into her white Coach purse and pulled out her jar of homemade hot pepper powder and sprinkled it on the chicken.

"Really?" Anne asked, looking over. "The chicken isn't fantastic enough without that?"

CC smiled and said, "It makes everything better."

After dinner, they walked along the boardwalk and darted in and out of the tiny shops. They watched craftsmen making their wares. CC thought about Ida's plight and how she could help. But most of all she thought about the man from the train.

Chapter Fifteen

Stepping off the elevator, Anne glanced up and down the long, narrow hallway of the high-rise office building on LaSalle Street. Etched on the double glass doors were the names, "Berman and Tabor, Attorneys at Law." Anne had only met with Jon Berman once before to review Sybil's will. Berman was handling Sybil's estate.

She opened the door and was greeted by a perky young law student, Kimberly, who was encased behind a wooden reception desk. "I have a meeting with Mr. Berman," Anne said.

"Yes, hi, Miss Hillstrom, Mr. Berman will be right out. Have a seat please."

A few minutes later, the short balding fifty-ish attorney came out to greet her. Shaking her hand, he said, "Anne, it's good to see you again. Follow me back to the conference room." Over Anne's shoulder, he said to the receptionist, "Kimberly, let me know when Mr. Stilton arrives."

Anne followed Jon Berman down the hallway, getting glimpses through the glass doors of other attorneys consulting with clients or poring over law books. She didn't think anyone was having a good time today. Anne wasn't having a good time. She knew that this moment was coming, but she was not looking forward to it. She stepped into the conference room after Jon Berman. He sat at the head of a long table which was surrounded by twelve leather chairs. Anne sat next to him on his right.

Jon pored through the files he had been carrying. He took his glasses out of his suit pocket and put them on the tip of his nose. He occasionally peeked over the tip of them at Anne just to remind her that he was sitting there. Finally, he closed his file and took his glasses off. He put them on top of the folder and sat back in his high back chair and swiveled towards Anne.

"Anne, your aunt's will is airtight. There's no room for misinterpretation. I don't see any grounds for contesting it," he said.

"The family is really upset. They feel that Aunt Sybil was not in her right mind." Anne tugged at her suit jacket. It was too tight.

"Anne, it's very difficult to contest a will. They'd have to prove that she wasn't of sound mind when she signed it, and they'd have to have evidence from a medical professional. I know that's not the case. I drafted the will for her, and she signed it a few weeks ago. She seemed fine to me."

"Why did Aunt Sybil wait so long to draft her will? She was 85 years old."

"Actually, she did have a will in place many years ago. I wasn't her attorney at that time. She contacted me a few months back and said that she wanted to write a new will. She was very specific about her wishes to have you act as executor and that her estate would be donated to the Field Museum."

"I think that's why the family is contesting it. They can't understand why she'd leave everything to the Museum. She's already given them our family heirlooms—Viking swords and jewelry." Anne paused. "I hadn't seen Aunt Sybil for at least three years. I kept meaning to visit, but either she was traveling or I was working. You know how it is. You just mean to get together with someone and things get in the way. To be honest with you, she wasn't always the easiest person to be around. Especially the past few years."

"When I went to her house a few months back, she seemed very nervous," Jon Berman said. "She insisted that the new will needed to be done quickly. Was your aunt sick?"

Anne shook her head. "Not that I know of."

"This is between you and me. I had to go to her house because she didn't want to come downtown. When I knocked on the front door, I heard her unlock the door and then I heard something heavy being dragged from behind it. When I walked in, I saw that she'd been using a heavy cement Christmas tree stand to barricade the door."

"I know that tree stand. When I was a little girl, we used it for our Christmas tree." Anne had wondered what had happened to it. She hadn't recalled seeing it at Sybil's house.

"When I asked about it, she shrugged me off," Jon Berman said. The buzzer sounded in the room. "The other attorney should be here now. Let me do the talking," he said to Anne.

Kimberly opened the door and led a sharply dressed young attorney into the room. He was followed by Suzanne, Jack, Uncle Dick, Aunt Sharon and a few other Hillstroms. They all took places at the large conference table across from Anne. The two attorneys shook hands and introduced themselves. Anne never stopped staring across the table at Suzanne and Jack.

Suzanne lowered her eyes. She couldn't bring herself to look back at Anne. Jack sat with a smirk on his face. He was wearing the same Vikings jersey that he'd worn to the anniversary party.

"Mr. Stilton and I spoke on the phone yesterday. We thought it might be best for us all to meet in person,"

Jon Berman said to the group. "After reviewing your Great Aunt's will, I can see no reason to contest it."

Mr. Stilton reached into his briefcase, which he'd plopped onto the table as Berman was speaking. "I have signed statements from nine blood relatives of Sybil Hillstrom. All of them state that Sybil had showed signs of dementia and paranoia for the past few years. In the past few months, she had become a shut in, not answering calls or leaving the house."

"How would they know? No one ever went to visit her," Anne interrupted. "No one called her." She looked around at her family members. "I'm as bad as the rest of you. I'll be the first to admit it. How can you say she wasn't right? You didn't know her."

"I saw her. I saw her three weeks ago," Jack said. "I was in town doing a job. Suzy wanted me to stop in and see her. I noticed some boards were loose on her front porch. The whole porch needed to be fixed. I offered to do the job for cost and she never paid me."

"I can understand why she never paid you after seeing the shoddy work you did at my house," Anne said. Mr. Berman put his hand on Anne's arm to stop her.

"You don't have any medical records or doctor's testimony to indicate that Miss Hillstrom was anything other than eccentric, do you, Mr. Stilton? There's no law against that," Mr. Berman said.

Jack stood up and pounded the table. "That old bitch was crazy and she deserved what she got."

Suzanne jumped up and pushed Jack back into his chair. "Shut up. Just shut up. I don't want to do this!" she screamed. "I loved Sybil. She doesn't deserve any of this." Suzanne started crying and ran out of the conference room. Anne ran out after her.

They stood in the hallway. Suzanne buried her face in her hands, sobbing and gasping for air. "Suzy, just catch your breath. It's okay," said Anne, putting her arm around her cousin.

"It's not okay. Nothing's okay," Suzanne struggled to speak through her tears.

Anne pulled a lace handkerchief out of her pocket and handed it to Suzanne, who held it to her eyes. "Thanks," Suzanne sniffled.

"Take a deep breath and we can talk," Anne said.

"I can't live with him anymore, but I feel trapped. I've got the kids, no home. I've got no job, no money."

"I know," Anne said.

"What am I going to do? After what just happened, I can't be alone with him," Suzanne said.

Anne grabbed Suzanne by the shoulders, locking eyes with her. "You can't live with him anymore. You have to leave him right now. He's going to hurt you— or worse—he's going to hurt the kids."

Suzanne rolled up her sleeve, looking at the floor too ashamed to admit it was true. Her arm was badly bruised and cut. She raised her red-stained puffy eyes to Anne's.

Anne fought to hold back the tears. "I know, honey. I know what you've been going through. I'm ashamed that I didn't try harder to stop it."

"You tried. I wouldn't listen."

Anne smiled, her whole face lit up. "Everything's going to be okay."

They walked back into the conference room. Suzanne sat next to Anne across from Jack. Suzanne was wearing the diamond and emerald Viking Queen's brooch that Sybil was supposed to be wearing in her casket.

Jack stared, angry and confused at the same time. "What's going on here?"

Mr. Berman said, "Part of Sybil Hillstrom's last wishes were that Anne be her executor. As executor, she has the power to decide who receives her most valuable possession—the Viking brooch."

"She was buried in that brooch. I saw her at the cemetery wearing the damn brooch in her coffin," Jack said.

"Sybil wanted all her loved ones to believe that she was taking the brooch with her," Anne said. "Her exact words in the will are, 'the brooch should go to the one who wants it the least, but who deserves it the most.' I believe Suzanne deserves it the most and now she has it."

"The rest of the antiques were sold at her estate sale. The proceeds will go to the Field Museum." Mr. Berman reached into the accordion file and pulled out some papers. "Suzanne, I need your signature on these." He passed the papers to her along with a black fountain pen.

"What are these?" Suzanne asked, skimming through the legal jargon.

"The will stipulates that the owner of the brooch also receives the deed to the house and a monthly allowance of $4,000 for maintenance." He read from the will in front of him.

"My name's on the deed already?" Suzanne said. "Why?"

"I knew the minute that Mr. Berman told me about Sybil's wishes and the wording in the will, just who deserved the brooch and the house," Anne said. "Your children should have the same memories that you and I have playing in that house."

"Damn, that's what I'm talking about," Jack said. "Finally, something that makes sense. Suzy, everything's going to be okay now."

"Yes, me and kids will be okay." Suzanne stared him right in the eye.

"What do you mean? Me and the kids?"

"We're moving into the house. You're not. I'm done with you." She turned to Mr. Berman. "Do you know a good divorce attorney?"

Jack jumped up again and tried to reach for his wife across the table. Uncle Dick held him back. "This isn't over!" Jack screamed. He glared at Anne, his bulging eyes about to pop out of his face, his biceps pushing against Uncle Dick. "This is all your fault, Anne! This isn't over!"

Chapter Sixteen

Saturday morning, CC's phone rang, rousing her from her sleep. The train whistle faded into the strident ringing of the phone. "Hello, Ms. Muller? CC? It's Helen Bradley from the *Daily Star*," the voice on the other end said.

CC cleared her foggy head and sat up. "Yes, Helen, how are you?"

"Sounds like I woke you. I'm sorry."

"No, it's all right."

"Just wanted to let you know we spoke with Mr. Talcott. This guy is a piece of work. When we confronted him, he admitted he might have made a mistake. He returned Ida's money and took the bears off the shelf. He didn't want any bad publicity."

"That's great news. Thank you," CC said and they hung up.

In small towns, word of mouth spreads quickly. Ida had told everyone she met about how Anne and CC had helped her with the bear. When CC blogged about the trip to Michigan, she received over 40 comments—the most she'd ever had in one day. Some were about Ida and the article about Talcott's collections, but even more were from people asking her to either authenticate or find something for them. CC scribbled notes on the pad she kept next to her computer.

Scanning the listings on estatesales.net, CC saw one promising listing that might be worth their time. She picked up the phone to call Anne.

Recognizing the number on her caller ID, Anne answered, "Hi, CC."

"Hello, Annie," CC said from the other end of the phone line. "I was finishing writing about our trip to Amish Acres. They mentioned our blog in *The Daily Star* article about Ida, and you won't believe this! We got over 40 comments."

"That's great," Anne said.

"It is great, but a lot of people are asking for our help. There's a woman from Holland who's looking for a Rosenthal plate. There's a man from Hobart looking for a pre-World War II Martin guitar," CC said, skimming through the comments.

"Why are they asking us? Why don't they just go to eBay or auctions?" Anne said.

"Most of them are nervous about purchasing items without the help of an expert eye, especially after reading about Ida," CC said. "I guess they feel they can trust us."

"That's great. Make a list. Let's go shopping."

"That's the other reason I called. Do you have any plans for this Saturday?" CC continued.

"Not as far as I know. What's up?" Anne replied.

"Something right up your alley. There's an estate sale in Sauganash," CC said. An old established neighborhood on Chicago's far north side, Sauganash residents teetered on the edge of the North Shore. Most residents believed they *were* the North Shore, but the true North Shorians had something else to say about it.

"What's at the sale?" Anne asked, perking up.

"Lots of furniture, jewelry, crystal—the pictures look high end, very collectible. And she collected bears," CC said

"I am so there, CC. Pick me up at seven," Anne said with a renewed enthusiasm in her voice.

That Saturday, on the way to the sale at Sauganash, Anne and CC stopped at a few garage sales they spotted along the way. Anne was on a mission to find the items on the growing list of requests from their *fans* as CC called them. CC hoped that when the time came for Anne to part with her purchases she'd be able to.

Noticing a large sign advertising a rummage sale on the corner of Pulaski Road, CC turned down a side street. They could hear the sounds of Polish music before even arriving in front of a church. This north side Chicago neighborhood consisted of a large Polish population. Outside of Warsaw, Chicago boasted the largest population of Polish people in the world. CC hoped to find something on their list.

The church parking lot was closed to parking, its blacktopped surface lined with individual tents, similar to a flea market. In the church's side yard, children were playing soccer. A food truck was parked selling Polish specialties including Kielbasa and sauerkraut, cabbage rolls and potato pancakes.

After quickly scanning items at the first table, Anne and CC walked away. It had been a large collection of children's toys, clothes and worn shoes. Not worth their time. The next tent had a long table cluttered with household items including glasses, pots and pans and mismatched silverware.

CC and Anne walked up and down the tables, looking carefully at the selection. At one table, they found a shoebox holding a mishmash of jewelry. CC sorted through it and pulled out what appeared to be a medallion. "Anne, look at these. They're scapular medals," CC said, holding them up to Anne. One side of the medal bore an image of Jesus. "It's marked *medalik szkaplerzny*. That's Polish for *scapular*." CC turned the medallion over and they could see the Virgin

Mary. "It's seen normal wear from being rubbed over the years. This has to date back to the early 1900s."

Anne picked one up and rubbed it between her fingers. "What kind of metal is this?"

"It's aluminum."

"It can't be worth a lot if it's aluminum."

"Actually, during that time period, aluminum was very valuable. It was worth a lot of money."

"What do you think we should offer?" Anne asked, sorting though the box, pulling out similar medals.

CC reached into her purse and pulled out her reporter's notebook. Scanning down the list, she remembered the name John Wilson. "Anne, Mr. Wilson—he's in Kalamazoo. He collects war medals and medallions. He's looking for European medallions. This might cover both. The Polish soldiers carried these into battle in World War I and II for protection."

"Let's get them then," Anne said.

Taking the medals to the woman holding the cash box, Anne and CC negotiated a price for the entire box. Anne slipped one into her pocket, hoping CC would not notice.

CC stopped to listen to the polka band and watch the folk dancers in their colorful native costumes. She noticed a table set up in front of a rusty delivery truck. Its faded lettering read, "Lock Service." A large elderly man sat on a folding chair behind the table, smoking a rolled cigarette. CC walked over. The table was piled high with padlocks, lock-picking tools, and combination locks, some new, some very old. CC stopped when she saw the padlock. It was an 1880s Trenton lock and hardware. CC held the cool metal in her hands and looked at him. He smiled. "You know your locks. That is a John Chinaman. Do you know the story?"

CC did but let him continue.

"It's called a story lock because of the image depicted on it. A Chinese fellow is attempting to steal a flask of whiskey through the window. The shopkeeper's dog catches him and bites his ankle. The lock was used as a restraining lock to lock up thieves," he explained.

"It's a beautiful example of their work. It's in great shape," CC said. "I'd love to have it. And this is the original key, isn't it?"

He nodded and rolled up another cigarette.

CC couldn't quite place his accent, but she'd smelled his tobacco before. It smelled Turkish. She picked up another lock. It was a 1910 post office combination lock used on mailbags. It was a five-cylinder model which was pretty rare. She gently spun the cylinders, which rotated smoothly. "I cleaned that one just recently," the man said.

"How much are you asking for these?"

"Why don't you start a pile? I think you're going to be here a while."

CC knew she was going to have to pay dearly for this. There was no hiding her enthusiasm. She made a large pile of the locks on the table. When she was done, CC made the calculations in her head. She knew she had to start at least at five hundred dollars. She didn't want to insult him, but she also wanted a good deal. Antique locks were on her list, but these would probably stay in her collection. She'd worry about that later. She took another whiff of the tobacco again and realized it wasn't Turkish. "Kolko Struva."

"Very good." He smiled and nodded. "You speak Bulgarian."

CC laughed. "No, I'm sorry I don't, but I finally recognized the accent. The tobacco had me fooled. I thought it was Turkish."

He shook his head. "God, no. I'm Bulgarian. Eleven hundred for everything," he said.

"I couldn't give you more than $400."

"That's not enough. The story lock is worth more than that by itself."

"$450?"

"You're a very nice lady, and I appreciate you speaking Bulgarian." He bit the tip of his cigarette and spat it out on the ground. "Tell you what, you make it $500 and I will give you something special for free." He got up and went into his van. He came back holding a large ring of skeleton keys. "These keys are very special. Some of these I cut myself. They will fit almost any padlock."

"Deal," CC said. She shook his hand and gave him her cash. She wrapped everything up in a large grocery bag and went to find Anne. She found Anne covered in powdered sugar, a large plate of kolacky in her hand.

"We have go to the sale in Sauganash. It ends soon," CC said.

Later, when they arrived in Sauganash, they pulled up to a brown brick bungalow on Chicago's far north side. It was typical of Chicago's 1920s homes and similar to Anne's. They walked up the cement steps and onto the porch. The front door was open, so they walked in. The home boasted its original oak wood trim and a brick fireplace. The oak floors creaked underneath their feet.

Anne was intoxicated by the smell of antiquity. CC headed directly for the basement. It smelled musty, a scent not unpleasing to CC. Ductwork and electrical conduit twisted its way along the open rafters down below ground. There was an eight-foot long homemade pine bar with four plush stools. CC sat down, staring at the eight-foot long beveled mirror that hung behind a hundred or so assorted bottles of whiskeys, liquors and vodkas. *Somebody had a great time in this basement*, CC thought. Next to the bottles were German beer steins, a bowling pin whiskey decanter and a little 1960s Hawaiian girl who could be coaxed to hula and shake your drink if you put a quarter in a slot. CC wanted everything. She thought about the scene from one of her favorite scary movies, *The Shining*. At first, it was fun talking to the ghostly bartender. Then she remembered the rest of the movie and jumped off the barstool quickly.

She went into the furnace room where there was a long steel cabinet that ran the length of the wall next to the oil boiler. The long skinny wooden drawers were filled with rusty tools. There were 20 mason jars filled with assorted screws, nuts and bolts, and nails. Attached to the top of the counter was an old hand-cranked vise. Above it, on the wall, a rusty handsaw hung. CC said out loud, "Somebody had a good time in here, too." She caught the attention of the estate sale employee working the basement and negotiated a price for all the items. The employee helped her carry them upstairs to the living room.

Anne went upstairs to one of the three small bedrooms. In the third bedroom, she found a collection of bears, ranging from beanie babies to a giant stuffed panda. In the middle was a small, perfectly cared for Steiff bear. Anne checked the button tag on its ear and the corresponding tag on its chest. Both looked to be original and intact. The only wear the bear showed was from being loved a lot. The fur was a bit matted where some little girl had held it close to her heart. Maybe it belonged to the owner when she was a little girl. No matter its story, it deserved to be loved.

CC poked her head in the bedroom. She was carrying German beer steins. "Anne, check these out. These are pre-World War II from Oktoberfest in Munich. They're awesome!"

Anne turned around to look at CC. Anne held up the bear so CC could see it.

"It's perfect." CC pulled out her iPhone, snapped a picture and then emailed it to Ida.

Feeling satisfied with their day's purchases, they stopped for lunch at Portillo's, a famous Chicago chain known for its Italian beef and hotdogs. Anne was not able to stay on her low carb diet. With all the excitement going on, she ordered a beef and cheddar croissant, *wet*—as true Chicagoans call *extra gravy*. She complemented the order with fresh-cut onion rings.

CC ordered a salad and a glass of water. She gave Anne a disapproving look at her choice of lunch.

"Really, after all that's happened, you're going to begrudge me a little comfort food?" Anne asked, taking a large bite out of her soppy sandwich.

CC didn't say a word, pulling her mason jar out of her purse and sprinkling it onto her salad. "It makes everything better," CC said before Anne could even comment.

Anne paused long enough to take the first bite of her chocolate cake.

"You know why Portillo's cake is so moist, don't you?" CC asked. "It's because they add mayonnaise to the batter."

Anne just nodded her head, her mouth full of chocolate cake.

After dropping Anne off at her house, CC went home and walked Bandit. Taking out their day's purchases, she photographed the items they'd found that were on the list and mailed them off to the various requesters. She then blogged about their day's adventures.

There was a new comment waiting for her. CC read it, "Hi, I'm Martha Thart, a freelance writer for the *Chicago Tribune*. My aunt, Susan, who summers in

New Buffalo, sent me the story about you and the bear. I pitched it to our feature editor, and she gave me the go-ahead to write your story. I'd like to arrange an interview."

CC hadn't expected this level of interest, but she was interested. She wrote back, "I work close to Tribune Tower. Could we meet for lunch somewhere on Michigan Avenue?"

She was tired, but she'd promised herself she would write five pages every night of her novel-in-progress. It had been ten years in the making now. She'd started writing it while she was still married. She found it a good release from reality. It had started out as a mystery about a journalist who solved murders and towards the end it became more of a romance novel. Romance was what she'd been missing in her marriage and in her life.

Chapter Seventeen

The phone rang, startling Anne from her thoughts. Looking at caller ID, she didn't recognize the number but decided to answer it anyway. "Hello," she said tentatively.

"Hello, Miss Hillstrom. This is Detective Towers," the British voice said on the other end.

"Oh, Detective Towers, how are you? You can call me Anne." She sat up in her chair. "What did you find out about my ring?"

"I went to Metro Sales and talked to the owner, Seth. He claims he bought the ring from a homeless man who said he found it on the street. He couldn't remember what the guy looked like, and he didn't have an ID," Towers said.

"There must be something you can do," Anne said.

"I spoke with the Glencoe police. The ring wasn't reported stolen, and without a bill of sale, there's no way to prove that it belonged to your aunt."

Anne was quiet for a moment. "Can I have my ring back?"

"Of course, Miss Hillstrom." He paused, and then said, "It's at the station. You can come sign for it. Or, it's my day off; I could meet you somewhere."

Anne half listened to Detective Towers. She was thinking about her aunt and the day she'd found her dead on the floor. She was thinking about the ring. She wasn't going to let this go. She owed it to Sybil. "Excuse me?" Anne asked, her train of thought screeching to a stop.

"I said, Anne, would you like to meet me for lunch? I can bring your ring."

"That would be fine."

As Detective Towers was talking, Anne's call waiting clicked. She saw CC's face. "I have to go. I have another call."

The line for Paradise Pup was long as always. It was well worth it. No one in line complained about waiting. They made the best charbroiled half-pound burgers in the Chicago area. The trick was grilled onions, Merkt's sharp cheddar cheese, German rye bread and an owner addicted to quality. Anne stood next to Detective Towers. Their difference in stature was almost comedic, yet they seemed very comfortable next to each other. Anne was surprised to see Detective Towers in his day-off clothes—white linen shorts and a salmon-colored polo shirt. For the first time, Anne thought, *this guy is kind of cute.*

When it came her turn to order, she ordered a half-pound cheeseburger with extra grilled onions and the loaded fries topped with Merkt's cheese, bacon and sour cream. Detective Towers smiled and ordered the same. Anne pulled out her wallet. "Put that away. I've got this," Detective Towers said.

They gathered their food and sat at a metal table outside the small building. A red and white umbrella provided coverage from the afternoon sun.

"How'd you find this place?" Anne asked.

"About two years ago, I was doing security at the Allstate Arena Theater. Oasis concert."

"Really? I like them. What ever happened to them? They were quite good," Anne said.

"Yes, they were quite good. One of the Rosemont officers working security told me about this place. Since then, I've come here at least once a week."

Detective Towers unwrapped his steaming burger. He took a bite and continued, "I'm sorry about the ring. I wish I could have found more information about it." He took the ring out of his pocket and handed it to her.

Anne watched a little dollop of ketchup on his cheek bounce as he talked. She found it rather charming. "You know," she said, "after we got off the phone, I remembered that on the way to the pawnshop, a homeless guy came up to me asking for money. He said he was trying to buy some shoes. His shoes were tattered up. He said he'd just been released from the 51st street station."

"Would you recognize him if you saw him again?"

"Yes, he made an impression on me." Anne dipped her fry in the cheese. Anne described the homeless man to Nigel Towers, right down to the color of his shoelaces. Her eye for detail had been honed by years of antique hunting.

"I'll check to see if anyone matches his description," Detective Towers accented his sentence by sticking his tongue out the corner of his mouth and catching the ketchup dollop.

"I have to know about the accent. Obviously you're British. How'd you wind up as a Chicago cop?"

"I was born in Liverpool. My father was a lieutenant in Scotland Yard. He wasn't around a lot growing up," Detective Towers said. "I spent more time with my mum. She loved American movies. We spent a lot of weekends at the cinema. Many black and white classics—*Casablanca* and *Bringing up Baby*. Our favorite movie was *The Maltese Falcon*."

"I love that movie," Anne interjected, sipping her Oreo cookie shake.

"It's ironic. My father was in one of the world's most famous detective departments, but I learned everything about police work from watching American films."

"Is that why you came to America?"

"Oh, no. My father was killed in the line of duty when I was twelve. My mum's sister married an American living in Chicago. As you might imagine, my mum had a pretty rough go of it after my dad died. We came here to live with them." He paused. "What about you? Tell me about Anne Hillstrom."

Anne took another sip of her Oreo cookie shake. "Not much to tell. I was born in the Midwest and went to school. I became a research chemist at Ebbort Labs. I've been working there for 25 years now."

"Chemist. That must be fascinating work."

Anne looked up, wearing a bit of a Hitler Oreo shake moustache. "Not so much. Not so much."

Nigel motioned to his lip, hoping she'd catch the gentle reference.

"I mostly test like pesticides, insecticides," she continued. "A lot of compound chemicals."

"Does that make you happy?"

Anne stopped gnawing on her French fry. It had been a while since someone had asked her that question. She couldn't remember ever being asked that question. In fact, it had been many years since she'd asked herself that question. She wiped the shake off the top of her lip with her napkin. "It's not what I started out wanting to do with my life."

"What did you want to do?"

"Don't laugh at me but when I was little I used to pretend I was Nancy Drew or Miss Marple in search of clues to solve mysteries. I always liked putting puzzles together." She stopped and thought before continuing, "The only puzzles I solve now involve emulsions and chemical reactions. Not exactly the stuff dreams are made of."

"I'm sure you're quite good at what you do," Nigel said.

"Thank you," replied Anne.

She cleared off the pile of napkins and their empty food on the table, disposing of it in the nearby garbage can. "Thanks for lunch. It was really good," Anne said.

Bumping his head on the umbrella, Towers struggled to get his praying mantis legs out from under the table. It made Anne laugh and the detective blushed. The awkward goodbye turned into a pleasant one.

Chapter Eighteen

CC was on deadline but she didn't want to cancel her lunch interview with Martha. She wrapped up the story she was working on. She ran the few short blocks to Boston Blackie's, a well-known Chicago hamburger joint. Scanning the lunchtime crowd, she recognized Martha, based on her description, sitting in a booth. CC gave her a quick wave and hurried over to the table, sitting down and catching her breath.

"CC, thank you so much for meeting me," Martha said, introducing herself.

"Thanks for your interest in my blog."

Martha pulled out a reporter's notebook. "Do you mind if I take notes?"

"No, not at all." CC shifted in her seat, suddenly feeling uncomfortable being on the opposite side of the notepad.

"I wanted to find out about your blog. It's called 'From the Estate'?"

"Yes, it's about me and my friend, Anne; we travel around to estate sales and share our experiences with our readers."

"Anne?" Martha questioned.

"Anne Hillstrom. We've been friends forever. Anne and I love treasure hunting."

"Tell me more about the treasure hunting." Martha scribbled notes furiously.

"When we were in college and didn't have any money, we started going to flea markets, rummage sales and then learned about estate sales. We were quickly hooked."

"What is it about estate sales that you enjoy?"

"For me, it's the thrill of the hunt. You never know what you're going to find, and I especially like handling antiques."

"What is it about old things?"

"It's really about the craftsmanship. The quality of the pieces. You don't see that today because everything is machine made. The people who crafted these items took pride in their work. They started as apprentices and took years to hone their skills. These pieces were crafted by human hands, not a machine. It gives them a soul." CC paused and thought. "It's a way to go back in time. You're touching history, and if you're really lucky, you might find something so rare, even one of a kind, that might have been lost."

"What's the most interesting thing you've found?"

"That's a really interesting question." CC paused again. "Every item has its own personality. One that was dear to my heart reminded me of my father. We came to America from Germany when I was quite young, and I've been back to Germany several times. On one trip, I found a cuckoo clock in the village where my dad was born." CC looked at her watch. "I have to get back to work."

"Thank you so much. I'd like to get some photos of you and Anne for the article. Would it be possible to take them at an estate sale?"

"Sure; I'll send the address of the next sale we're going to go to." After shaking hands, CC got up and headed back to work.

Chapter Nineteen

Anne dreaded Monday mornings, Tuesday mornings, and Wednesday mornings. Thursdays weren't so bad; Fridays pretty good. She walked into the large multi-complex Ebbort Building. She passed through the security checkpoint, waving to the security guard, heading down the corridor to the sealed doors that housed her weekday home. With a swipe of her ID badge, the double stainless doors swooshed open.

She entered the clean room and donned her lab coat before going to her station. This week she was testing organic compounds for mosquito repellent. She shared the lab with two other chemists. Ebbort Labs' interest in mosquito abatement had increased as the threat of West Nile Virus had grown. Her part was just the first in a series of independent tests to validate preliminary research results. She really hoped it would work because she was tired of being bitten. The DEET and citronella candles were proving no match for these aggressive mosquitos. With all the flooding in the Midwest, it had been a really bad year. On her left arm alone, she had over five bites.

For the first time in a long while, she was actually interested in work. After working in silence for a few hours, she was interrupted by Sharon, her fellow chemist—a younger girl recently graduated from college. "Hey, how's the repellent going?"

"Honestly, DEET is still the best repellent but who wants to spray that on." Anne took off her safety glasses and looked at Sharon and said, "What works for me pretty well is a dryer sheet. It has to be scented. Just rub it all over your skin. It keeps off all but the most aggressive mosquitoes."

"Very interesting," said Sharon. "How was your weekend?"

"It was good," replied Anne. "I went to a sale. I found a beautiful Steiff bear. It was on my list."

"What list is that?" Sharon looked quizzically at her.

"Oh, my friend CC and I—you've met her—have a blog about our finds at estate sales. A lot of our fans have been writing to us looking for help finding items."

"Really? That's pretty cool. Maybe you can help me out," Sharon said.

"What are you looking for?" Anne asked, getting enthusiastic.

"My boyfriend and I are buying a loft off of Madison and Racine, not too far from the United Center. He wants to bring over all his furniture. Let me clarify that—his junk." Sharon leaned against Anne's table. "I'm trying to be fair about it. I told him he could pick three of his favorite possessions, but I get to okay them. Anne, you should see his taste. It's like he's still in a college dorm room."

Anne rubbed her chin and looked thoughtful. "Let me see. What's your style? What do you like?"

Sharon sat on the stool next to her. "I really love 1960s mod. I'd love to find an Andy Warhol, a real one. I inherited a couple Eames chairs and I'd like to decorate the whole loft around them."

"Eames chairs. Those are really valuable," Anne said. "I'll put you at the head of the list. I've got some ideas in mind for 1960s décor." Anne thought for a moment. "I might just have a few things in my garage. Give me a day or two." She had to decide if she was willing to part with one of her Formica kitchen tables or her avocado green stove.

"Thanks, Anne." Sharon stood up. "We're heading out to lunch. Do you want to join us?"

"Not today. I brought lunch," Anne said. She watched her coworkers walk out. Anne sat at her desk, nibbling her chicken salad sandwich, browsing through her eBay watch list. Anne took a couple bites and reached into her drawer, pulling out a Reese's peanut butter cup. "If I eat half the sandwich, I can eat the whole candy bar," she said to herself. She scrolled down her eBay watch list. The silver tea service that had started at $25 was now up over $100. Too bad; she couldn't spend that much right now. She had overextended herself again and was struggling to pay her monthly bills. She didn't tell CC because she didn't want a lecture.

After work, Anne headed to the police station to meet Nigel Towers. She sat in the viewing room as Nigel spoke with the homeless man who matched her description. It was definitely him. She watched through the glass and listened intently.

"Tell me, Mr. Findle, you say that some guy came up to you and asked you to hock this ring?" Nigel put the ring on the table.

The homeless man touched the ring and said, "Yep, yep; that's it. That's the ring."

"What did this man look like?"

"I don't know—just a middle-aged white guy, kind of greasy." The homeless man's leg bounced up and down with a nervous energy.

"What do you mean by *greasy*?"

"He seemed kind of off. He didn't seem right, you know what I mean?"

"Did he say why he wanted you to pawn the ring?"

"He said that he'd lost a lot of money at the track and he wanted to sell his wedding ring. He'd told his wife that he lost it. He didn't want her to find out.

That's why he wanted me to go inside the pawnshop. He said he'd split the money with me whatever I got from the pawn shop guy."

"What happened after you pawned the ring?"

"I got $50 for it. I thought that was pretty good. The pawn shop guy thought it was fair, but the guy in the alley was mad. He said the ring was worth much more than that, and he roughed me up a little bit and stiffed me. He didn't give me a dime. You know, I shouldn't have trusted him; he was wearing a Vikings jersey in Chicago. Who wears a Vikings jersey in Chicago?"

Anne jumped out of her seat. Nigel finished up with Mr. Findle and walked into the viewing room where Anne was dancing around. "Nigel, the Vikings jersey! I know who it is! My cousin Suzanne's husband, Jack, was wearing a Vikings jersey last time I saw him. He did some work for my Aunt Sybil. I bet you he stole the ring when he was at her house. I just know he did. He's that kind of guy."

"Greasy?"

"Yes, greasy; that's a good way to describe cousin Jack."

"Do you have an address for him?"

"No; he and Suzanne split up recently, and he took off. I don't know where he is now. He's from Minnesota. His parents live in St. Paul; maybe you could check there."

Nigel smiled at Anne. He appeared to feel good that there was something he could do to help her.

By the time she got home, it was after 8 p.m., and Sassy was not pleased. "Okay, Sassy, I know you're starving."

Sassy paid no attention and headed to the kitchen. She waited on the shelf above the kitchen table. Anne reached up, pulling Sassy off the shelf. "We've talked

about this. I don't want you knocking anything over."
Anne placed Sassy on the floor next to her food dish.

After Sassy was fed, Anne called her bank to check on her balance. The news wasn't good as she'd suspected.

Chapter Twenty

CC's trip to New York to cover the steel shipbuilding conference had exhausted her. She didn't even have time to blog. She'd returned home on Friday and had sat down at her computer. There were hundreds of comments awaiting her. She sifted through them and added their requests to her list. One comment was from Ida. She paused to open it. It was a picture of Ida holding her new granddaughter and the Steiff bear. "Thank you," Ida had written. CC sat back and smiled.

Then she started writing her next blog post, "Dear Friends, last week, Anne and I went to a sale in Sauganash, which is a neighborhood on the north side of Chicago. Old oak trees line both sides of the streets, draping over the middle. Jumbo brick bungalows are beautifully restored, " she wrote as the phone rang.

CC picked it up. "Hello?"

"CC, it's Anne," the voice said.

"What's up, Anne? I just got back."

"I was at the police station with Nigel who was questioning the homeless guy who pawned my ring," Anne said. "He said the guy he got it from was wearing a Minnesota Vikings jersey."

"And?"

"Jack. Jack was wearing a Vikings jersey at Aunt Sharon's anniversary party."

"You think Jack stole your ring?"

"Nigel's going to look for him. Oh, and Mr. Ripley is having another sale tomorrow in Highland Park. I think we should go. The pictures look fantastic," Anne said, barely containing her enthusiasm.

CC gazed at the growing list in front of her. "Sure; what time do you want to go?"

"It starts at 9 a.m., and I want to get there first thing. Should I come to your house and we can go from there?"

"Sounds good." CC hung up the phone She emailed the reporter with the address of the sale, in case she wanted to send a photographer to the Packwall estate sale as she'd indicated.

Then she went back to writing her blog. Before closing her computer, she scanned her list of requests. Most of them were pretty ordinary items. One item stood out. A friend of Ida's, Tony Tedesco, was looking for a 1929 Baglietto ship bell. "Baglietto," she mused. "I've never heard of that."

She Googled *Baglietto* and read out loud to Bandit. "Baglietto is a shipyard that builds fine mega-yachts, motor yachts and speedboats in its home country of Italy. The company was founded as a boat builder in 1854. They relocated to a waterfront wood boat building plant around 1890. During the 1920s, they mostly made government boats and seaplanes. By the 1950s, they were known for their speedboats as well as motor yachts and sailboats. Baglietto uses mahogany, iroko and teak for their wood boats," she finished reading. "Interesting." She shut down the computer and headed outside with Bandit.

Chapter Twenty-One

The next morning after stopping for Starbuck's to fuel CC's caffeine habit, they headed to Highland Park, a quaint little upscale community surrounded by large forest preserves.

"Martha, that reporter from the *Tribune* who I told you about, is going to meet us. She wants to talk to you and take our picture," CC said.

"Why is that?" Anne asked.

"It's for that story she's doing on the blog. They wanted to get a photo of us at a sale. I emailed her with the information about today's sale."

CC turned down a long side street that ended at Lake Michigan. The homes here were palatial and situated on large lots. This particular home was a white Colonial with green shutters. Parked in the driveway in front of the house was a vintage Rolls Royce Silver Cloud with a *For Sale* sticker on the windshield. Large purple Jackmannii clematis wrapped around the marble pillars supporting the wraparound porch. Massive pink clusters of hydrangea flower balls outlined the elevated deck. CC stopped to examine them—not a single hole in the leaf. Whatever Nancy Packwall had been using had kept the caterpillars and other creepy crawlers off the plant. She admired the Sarah Bernhardt peonies, soaking in their aroma.

Anne darted past CC to jump in the line that extended from the front door and was winding into the driveway. "I love this house," Anne said to CC.

"It's built in the Greek revival style that was very popular in the antebellum south," CC said. "Architects in the area started copying the design after soldiers came back from the Civil War."

The history lesson flew past Anne. CC had a tendency to tell people much more than what they wanted to hear. Once again, Anne saw Betsy Buttersworth at the front of the line. Just once, she wanted to get to a sale before her.

At exactly the stroke of 9 a.m., the green front door opened. Mr. Ripley came out and counted, as people started filing in. As Anne and CC moved to the front of the line, Ripley held out his hand, blocking them. "That's it for now. You'll have to wait until some people leave," he said.

Anne wanted to argue, but she knew it was futile. She tapped her foot impatiently. She didn't like waiting. After what seemed like an eternity, several people filed out, carrying bags. Anne tried to peek in their bags as they walked by. Anne gave Mr. Ripley a perturbed look. He smiled and let them in.

They walked around the first floor. The 90-year-old woman, Nancy Packwall, who'd lived in the house, was a retired costume designer for campy B-grade horror movies from the 1950s and 60s. She'd moved back to Highland Park in the 70s. There were a lot of movie posters and memorabilia scattered throughout the main floor. In the living room, two locked glass cases held her collection of vintage jewelry, including a Harry Winston diamond necklace, some Tiffany chains and a Cartier emerald bracelet. Most of Mrs. Packwall's money had been made by outliving four husbands.

CC drifted to the jewelry case. She was always looking for unusual pieces to add to her collection. She especially admired Mexican and American Indian silver pieces. Out of the corner of her eye, she saw a sterling silver bracelet decorated with a large turquoise stone. After asking the woman guarding the jewelry case to see it, CC held it in her hand. She could see worn engraving that appeared to be a medical warning, but she couldn't make it out. To her, it made the bracelet even more interesting. She negotiated a price with the woman and asked her to hold it while she continued to shop.

She stepped out the sliding glass door that led onto a tumbled cobblestone patio, surrounded by daylilies, David Austin roses, and creeping phlox. She went over to smell a double delight hybrid tea rose with a pale pink center with a white exterior. At the edge of the patio, a curved wooden bridge traversed a koi pond. A rough cobblestone path, lined with native prairie tickseed and meadow sage, led to the back yard where there was a large glass greenhouse. She strolled over to take a look. The door was locked. She was able to peek in and see the beautiful orchids inside. CC sat on the green granite bench in front of the greenhouse. There was no *For Sale* sticker or price on the bench. It would look wonderful in her garden. She ran her hand along the cool, beveled edge. The foxglove and cone flowers would be blooming soon. It was very quiet and peaceful in this garden. The only scent that would make it even better would be French roast coffee and a smoldering Gitane. It had been years since she'd had her last cigarette. She'd smoked a lot when she was married; it had helped with the stress. There was something about coffee and a cigarette. She could almost smell the sickly sweet scent of tobacco now. She inhaled deeply. She did smell tobacco.

Standing up, she walked back up the path. From behind the large weeping willow tree, she saw Mr. Ripley smoking. She ducked behind the tree and made herself very small. She stood very still. She really shouldn't be in the backyard. She inhaled again and the scent was gone. CC waited a couple minutes before heading back to the house. As she turned around, she stepped out from behind the tree and bumped into Mr. Ripley.

He was standing very still. "You shouldn't be out here," he said.

CC gave him an uneasy smile and ran past him into the house.

Moving upstairs to the master bedroom, Anne thought it fitting for a Hollywood designer. Decorated in pink chintz, it had white French impressionist furniture. A silk dressing gown hung over the fainting chair. Putting the back of her hand to her forehead, Anne said to no one in particular, "Really, Rhett Butler, I do declare you overwhelm me. You're giving me the vapors." She fanned herself and swooned onto the chair. From this perch, she saw the opening to what appeared to be a closet.

She strolled into a massive walk-in closet. One wall held shelves of shoes, purses and hatboxes. Clothing hung from the rods on the other three walls. Anne rifled through the racks. She stopped and held her breath for a second. She recognized the pants immediately. The colorful pansy-festooned pants were from Nancy's last movie—the 1967 cult classic, *Bikini Blood Beach*. The Capri pants had been worn by a young Stevie Vann before she'd become a star. As Anne admired the craftsmanship, a hand flew past her grabbing them off the hanger.

She turned to see Betsy admiring her prize. "Okay, that's it, Buttersworth. I've had just about enough of you. You saw me looking at the pants. I found them first." Anne placed a hand on the pants.

Betsy interrupted her. "You hesitated and you lost. They're mine!"

"Not this time, Buttersworth!" Anne grabbed one of the pants legs and tugged. The tug of war didn't last long.

"Ladies, ladies! We could hear you arguing all the way downstairs," Mr. Ripley said, walking into the room. "What's going on here?"

"I was looking at these pants, planning to buy them. And she grabbed them right out of my hands," Anne said, maintaining her hold on the pants leg.

"That's not true. She wasn't holding them. They were on the hanger. The pants are mine," Betsy said, clutching her end.

"Ladies, we have to come up with a civil way to decide who can buy the pants. I wasn't here to see what happened, and, by the looks of it, I don't see either one of you are giving them up," Mr. Ripley said, staring at them sternly.

Both women stood fast, each holding a pants leg. After reflection, Mr. Ripley said, "I can't decide this for you. By the end of the day, whoever is holding the pants can have them."

Anne and Betsy gave each other a determined look and started out of the bedroom, each retaining their grip on the precious pants. The newly formed Siamese twins moved cautiously down the stairs into the foyer.

"I'm not letting go," Anne hissed.

Betsy muttered under her breath. "I've got all day. I've got no place to be."

For the next three hours, the two wandered around the house, picking up items with one hand while holding onto the pants with the other.

"Okay, this is getting really silly. Let me have the pants. Pick out any item you want and I'll pay for it," Betsy said.

"I don't want your charity. This isn't about the money. It's not even about the pants anymore. It's the principle," Anne said.

"For goodness' sake. I have to use the bathroom," Betsy said.

"No one's stopping you," Anne said.

Betsy shrugged it off. The two walked into the gourmet kitchen which had a rooster theme despite the contemporary stainless appliances. Roosters adorned the wall; ceramic roosters filled the shelf above the window; and the backsplash had roosters in the tiles.

Anne walked to the faucet and turned it on.

Betsy danced a little. "Turn that off," she said.

Anne sat down at the kitchen table.

"What are you doing?" demanded Betsy

"It's been a long day," said Anne calmly. "I'm going to rest here."

Betsy danced and fidgeted around behind Anne's chair. "Fine, they're yours!" Betsy said, letting go of the pants and stomping off.

Anne clutched the pants to her breast, caressing them. Looking out the garden window, she saw Mr. Ripley talking loudly to a well-dressed man. They seemed to be arguing. Anne walked to the back door and opened it slightly to hear.

"What happened to the spoon? Mr. Whitmore's nephew has been calling me everyday since the estate sale," the man said to Mr. Ripley.

"Like I told you on the phone, Banning, every item at the sale was marked either with a price or NFS. I've looked on my tally sheet. There were lots of silver spoons. I'm not sure which one he's talking about," Mr. Ripley said.

"Jared says it had some sentimental value—family heirloom or something. It wasn't supposed to be for sale, and now it's missing," Banning said.

"Ill check with my assistant and let you know. "Thank you for putting me in touch with Mrs. Kirby. I'll send you your usual finder's fee after we tally the proceeds from the sale."

"Call me when you find the spoon." Banning turned on his heel and walked across the lawn to a black Mercedes.

Spoon, huh? Anne thought to herself. She closed the door quietly. A tap on her shoulder made Anne nearly jump out of her skin. "Anne, Martha from the *Tribune* is here," CC said. Standing behind CC was a woman about their age, carrying a reporter's notebook and camera.

"Hi," Anne said, shaking the reporter's hand while maintaining her hold on the pants.

"You must be Anne. CC told me quite a bit about you when we talked the other day," Martha said. "Perhaps we can sit here and talk." The reporter pointed to the kitchen table. Anne sank back down on one of the chairs, and Martha sat across from her.

"I'll just stay here and listen if you don't mind." CC hovered in the background, leaning against the wall.

"CC says you are antique hunters. How'd you get interested in antiques?"

Anne thought for a moment. "My interest in antiques started early on. I used to spend the summers at my Great-Aunt Sybil's house. She was a collector of many things from stamps to jewelry to spoons. She would take me to sales with her. She taught me how to identify and authenticate antiques."

"Are there certain antiques you look for?"

"Of course—the more rare the better. Right now, we've been concentrating on a list."

"CC touched briefly on that. Tell me more about the list."

"People have been writing in to our blog, asking us to find things that they're looking for. Some are harder than others to find. We have a pretty good network of antique dealers, estate sale managers and so on that we've connected with over the years," Anne said.

"What are some of the items on the list?"

"They really vary. One woman is looking for a Rosenthal plate that matches the service her grandmother had. A guy is looking for a pre-World War I Martin guitar. Someone else wants a Mystery Date game. It runs the whole gamut," Anne said. "Get the list out, CC," Anne continued, looking over at CC who was still holding up the wall.

"That's not necessary," said Martha. "How about you personally? What catches your eye in an antique?"

Anne held up the pants. "I wouldn't call them antique, more vintage, but take these pants. They were worn by Stevie Vann, a starlet from the 1960s, and now they will be mine." From the corner of her eye, Anne saw Betsy Buttersworth watching the whole travesty. She did not look pleased.

"What would you say is the most unique item you've ever found?"

"Every item is unique in its own way. Touching something from the past connects you with history. It could be something as simple as a Victorian thimble to my Aunt Sybil's collection of Viking swords and jewelry," Anne said.

"That's an interesting way to look at antiques," Martha said, scribbling in her notepad.

Anne nodded. "Oh, yes, holding an antique in your hand brings you in touch with its history."

Martha checked her watch. "I have to get going, but I'd like to get a picture of you and CC. Maybe in front of the dining room table where all the crystal is displayed."

"Wait, I have to do something first." Anne ran out of the kitchen and into the living room. She paid the woman who was tallying purchases at the card table by the front door. Anne wrote out a check, hoping it wouldn't bounce.

"Can I have your phone number?" the woman asked Anne.

Anne rattled off her number and the woman jotted it down on the top of the check. "Thanks." Trying to look casual, Anne glanced around, saw a small doorway marked *Do Not Enter*. Opening the door slowly, she saw no one around. She darted in, closed and locked the door. She slipped on the pants. A perfect fit. She turned and gazed at herself in the mirror, admiring herself from every angle. Exactly like Stevie Vann, if she said so herself.

Opening the door slowly, she once again checked around before stepping out of the bathroom. Walking into the dining room, she saw CC standing in front of the crystal and china laden table. Martha was holding her camera up to her face. "Anne, those pants look perfect!" Martha said.

"Yes, they do, Anne." CC gave Anne a sharp look. "Where'd you get them?"

"Just now. Aren't they marvelous?" Anne twirled around.

"They're fabulous," Martha agreed with her. "Please stand next to CC."

Anne posed, sticking one leg out in front of the other as she'd seen contestants do on *America's Next Top Model*.

After Martha had finished taking her pictures, CC paid for her purchases. She and Anne then headed to the car with their bags. "Where'd you get those pants?" CC asked, holding a small bag.

"It's a long story. I'll tell you at lunch."

"I want to let the dog out. Let's go to my house. I'll make us something," CC said.

Anne thought about her checking account and remembered the check she'd just written. Lunch at CC's was a good idea, she realized.

CC looked in her fridge. She hadn't gone shopping since she'd gotten back. The only thing left was a few chicken breasts. She thought about her mom's smothered chicken recipe. Heating olive oil in a pan, she dredged the chicken breasts in flour and added salt and pepper and her extra spicy mix. She put the chicken breasts in the pan. In another pan, she melted some butter, added mushrooms and onions. She went out to the garden and grabbed some romaine, Early Girl tomatoes and chives to make a fresh salad. After the onions and mushrooms had caramelized, she added sour cream and allowed it to simmer.

Placing the chicken breast on a plate, she covered it with the mushroom/onion mixture and added the salad. "Anne, lunch is ready," she called downstairs to Anne who was looking at eBay on her computer. The silver set was now up to $200, way past her limit.

Anne went up to the table and sat down. CC poured them both a glass of white wine. "This looks fantastic, CC," Anne said, taking a bite of the chicken.

CC put her fork down. "Oh, I almost forgot. Our list has gotten bigger. We're now up to over 200 items to search for." She pulled the list out of her purse which was dangling off the back of the chair.

"You know if we're going to be putting all this time and effort looking for items for other people," suggested Anne, "don't you think we should charge them something for our trouble?"

CC thought about it for a moment. "I think it'd be okay to make a small profit, just enough to cover expenses."

"Yeah, just enough to cover expenses. That's all," Anne agreed. As Anne continued eating her chicken, CC read from the list.

"A 1929 Baglietto brass ship bell."

"Ship bell?" Anne looked up from her plate. "Let me think. I don't know what year it is, but I have a brass ship bell in my storage locker."

"What? What are you doing with a bell?" CC asked.

"I bought it when they shut down the Great Lakes Navy Base along with some office furniture and bunk beds."

"Really? Bunk beds?"

"Yeah, they're all in my storage locker," said Anne.

"Maybe we should take a ride to your place and go look at it."

The two rushed through the remainder of lunch, cleaned up and then headed ten miles west to Anne's storage locker. "It's locker #325, #425," Anne said, as she searched in her purse and pulled out a set of keys.

"How many storage lockers do you have?" CC asked, driving around the alleyway.

"Just the three." They pulled up in front of locker #532. Anne unlocked the padlock and opened the large overhead door. CC jumped as a box fell on top of her foot. The locker was overflowing with cardboard boxes, garbage bags and everything. There was no order to any of it.

"How in the world are you going to find a bell in this mess?" CC asked, moving the box.

"I know exactly where it is," Anne replied, climbing over a desk chair and squeezing past a metal footlocker, then pulling a moving blanket carefully off a teetering pile. There it was—the brass ship's bell. It was quite heavy, but Anne managed to retrieve it without doing too much damage to the stained glass windowpanes that surrounded it. She followed her steps backward over the pile and laid the bell at CC's feet with a flourish.

CC was still concentrating on the teetering piles of odd-sized boxes. "Really, Anne, three storage lockers like this?" CC examined the bell. "It wasn't a Baglietto but it was inscribed with *bella* in Italian. "I think this is pretty close," CC said. "It looks pretty old. It's in great shape."

While CC took pictures of the bell with her iPhone, Anne looked at the Formica table and avocado green stove. She opened the stove and looked inside. She twisted some of the knobs. "I don't know," she said out loud. "I really like this a lot. I think I could make it work in my kitchen."

"What are you talking about?" CC looked up.

"Sharon at work was looking for some furniture for her new place. She has a 1960s motif."

CC walked over and looked at the stove. "That would work. That's a 1960s Hotpoint. Did you know the sheet metal they used was from the Gary plant I told you about?"

"Okay. Good to know for next time," Anne said with a giggle. As they walked back to CC's car, Anne gave the stove one last look. It would take a lot for her to part with it.

Later that night, CC sent the pictures of the bell to Tony Tedesco. Then she sat down at her computer to write her next blog entry. "Dear Friends," she started as she sipped from her steaming hot French press coffee. "Today, Anne and I traveled to another fabulous sale run by Mr. Ripley. He is gaining quite the reputation for holding high-end sales. This sale was at the home of the former Hollywood costume designer, Nancy Packwall. I found this fantastic poster, which I will hang in my bathroom," CC wrote, uploading a picture of the colorful B movie framed poster.

"Anne found several things but the most important was a pair of flowered pants." Here CC uploaded a picture of the pants that she'd taken before Anne had left. "I have a feeling that we are going to be seeing much more of these pants so prepare yourselves."

As she was writing, Tony Tedesco's name popped up in the "waiting" comments section. She opened his comment and read, "The bell looks exactly like what I've been looking for. How'd you find it? And, how can I get it from you? How much do I owe you?"

She wrote him a quick reply, briefly explaining how she'd found the bell. She also said that she could drop the bell in the mail. His reply came back before she could shut down the computer.

"I'm in Chicago working at the Chicago Yacht Club. If you're in the city, I could meet you," he wrote back.

"I work in the city just a few blocks from the Yacht Club. I could bring it over on my lunch hour," she typed back quickly.

"That would be great. How about Tuesday?" he wrote back.

"Sure. I'll be there about noon," she typed back. With the plans confirmed, she shut down the computer and went to walk Bandit.

Chapter Twenty-Two

On Tuesday, CC walked past the long low white building set on the shore of Lake Michigan. Moving along the cement pier, she walked past the schooners and sailboats, looking for the one called *Annabella*. She stopped and asked a teenage boy who was scrubbing down the pier. He pointed to a 50-foot wooden sailboat.

As she walked up to the boat, Tony Tedesco came out of the cabin, wearing denim shorts and deck shoes. He brushed his long salt and pepper hair away from his eyes and wiped the sweat from his face with his t-shirt. He saw CC and put his t-shirt on. "CC, hi! I'm Tony," he said with a melodic Italian accent.

It's the man from the train, CC thought. She stared, not answering.

"You are CC, right?" Tony asked again.

"Yes, yes. Hi, Tony," CC stammered. She reached into her Trader Joe's bag and pulled out the brass bell that sparkled in the midday sun.

Tony jumped off the boat and took the bell from her hands, looking it over, smiling. "Yes, it's perfect. Great job, CC," he said, holding onto the bell.

"Is this your boat?" she asked.

"No, I'm just restoring it," he said. "The bell's for my boat which is docked in New Buffalo. That's where my marine shop is."

New Buffalo; that's what he was doing there, CC thought to herself, nodding.

Tony stopped and took a closer look at her. "Have we met before?"

"Not that I recall," CC said.

"Do you want to see the boat?" he asked.

"Sure." CC nodded.

"Careful; the planks are a little wobbly," Tony said, putting his hands around her waist, lifting her up and twirling her onto the boat. She felt like Beryl Grey dancing *Swan Lake* at age 15. "I've been regrouting the deck. Mahogany breathes really well, but with all the shifting, the grout becomes loose. This has been a three-month project so far," Tony said, showing her around the boat.

She recognized one of the tools she'd seen in the white pickup truck. "What's that for?" she asked, pointing at one of the irons.

"That's used to clear out the old grout between the mahogany planks."

"You do everything by hand?"

"That's really the best way to restore one of these old wooden boats. The craftsmanship is remarkable. All these planks were hand sawn and perfectly matched. You can see the slight bow which is normal in any plank. The bow is even throughout all the planks. Each piece was specially chosen so it would line up perfectly," Tony explained, pointing at the deck of the boat.

"It's beautiful work. I can see why it would take so long to regrout and refinish it," CC said.

"Yes; you need to treat these yachts with respect. Each one has a personality. You can feel it in the wood when you touch it."

CC smiled. She understood how Tony felt. She appreciated craftsmanship too. She'd spent her whole life admiring skilled steelworkers and metal cutters. She understood what it meant to build something with your hands. She could see the passion in his eyes when he spoke about the boat. The same passion she hoped she exuded when she spoke about steel.

"I've bored you. I've talked too long, haven't I?" Tony asked.

"No, no; it's quite interesting. Do you know how you can tell it's African mahogany versus Honduran?" CC asked.

He shrugged.

"African mahogany tends to have more ribbon striping."

"I never knew that."

"Yes, that's why it's more expensive, because it's more difficult to match," CC explained.

"I really appreciate you finding the bell and bringing it down here. How can I thank you?" While he was speaking, his hands danced and the sun reflected off his wedding band.

"You can start by paying me," CC said, her tone suddenly more businesslike than friendly.

"Of course." He reached in his pocket and pulled out a check. "Sure I can't buy you lunch? You're missing your lunch hour because of me."

"No, that's okay. I have a lot to do at the office. It was nice meeting you. Thanks for the tour." She turned quickly and headed down the gangplank. When she got to the bottom, she promised herself that she wouldn't turn around to see the man from the train again. This time she kept her promise.

She walked along the lakefront. It was a beautiful day. The seagulls danced overhead. The lake was very calm. The Chicago skyline was a glistening backdrop. She'd spent many nights dreaming about meeting the man on the train someday. About what that would be like. About what *he* would be like. And now she knew. She found herself walking out onto the horseshoe, as it was known. The horseshoe was a long cement pier curving partially back towards shore. It was lunchtime and fisherman were out trying their best to catch some lake perch. She strolled along, peeking in buckets to see who'd caught what. She walked to the end of the pier and sat on the edge, looking down at the 10-foot drop and the lake water crashing into the cement pillars. She stared across the lake and wondered if her double was sitting on another pier staring back at her. What was that CC like? Had *she* just met her man on the train? Was she turning 40 and alone? What would her life have been like if she hadn't married the wrong man at the wrong time? What would her life have been like if she hadn't thrown herself into her work and made it the most important thing in her life?

CC leaned back on her elbows and looked up at the powder blue sky. The air was sweet, fresh and cool. She could hear a radio turned to the Cubs' game. There was something about listening to baseball on the radio. Much better than watching it on TV. *The mind always paints better pictures than the eyes,* she thought.

Chapter Twenty-Three

Sassy was nipping at her heels; breakfast was late. Anne stumbled out of bed, fed her and then sank into her favorite chair. She switched on *Meet the Press*, her favorite show. She pulled the tarnished silver spoon out of her purse and held it in her hand. She got up, walked to the sink and pulled out a soft cloth. She might as well clean the spoon while catching up on her Sunday morning news shows.

She admired the ornate scrollwork on the spoon handle. It reflected a more elegant and genteel time. As she scrubbed, she noticed an interesting mark on the back of the spoon. She couldn't quite make it out. This would require a trip to CC's house, but first—the pants. She went into her closet where the pants were dangling from a silk hanger. Taking them off the hanger, she held them for a moment, admiring the craftsmanship. Then, she slid them on, reveling in the feel of the silky material against her legs.

She then went to grab her car keys. It seemed like her keys always had legs; they were never where they should be. She moved the stack of *National Geographics* from the 1950s, but they weren't under them. She inspected the stack of silk scarves she kept in a woven Longaberger basket, but they weren't there. After ten minutes of searching the usual hiding places, she opened the front door to go see if she'd left them in the car, and that's when she found them dangling from the keyhole.

Driving as fast as she could, she raced to CC's house in her Mercury Mystique.

Wearing a large straw gardening hat, CC was in her backyard, weeding her vegetable garden. Along with tomatoes, cucumbers and lettuce, CC grew peppers—not just ordinary peppers—but jalapeno, ghost peppers and, her new favorite, Carolina Reaper peppers. Tasty but extremely hot. The hotter the better for CC. She took the hottest of the peppers along with assorted herbs and spices from her garden and made her own seasonings. CC looked up, startled when she heard a *hello* coming from over the large wooden fence. Bandit barked excitedly. "Quiet, down, Bandit; it's just Anne. You know Annie."

Bandit apologized by rubbing his head against Anne's leg. Anne ran her hands through the dog's soft fur.

"Hi, Anne, I wasn't expecting you." CC pulled off her gardening gloves and put her trowel on the patio table.

"I was so excited about what I found, I had to show you! I had to run over right away to use your computer," Anne spat out breathlessly, flopping herself into one of CC's lawn chairs.

"What did you find? I don't recall you talking about shopping today." CC looked her friend over. "I see you're wearing *the pants*."

Anne stood up and did a quick turn. "Pretty good fit, don't you think?"

"Yes, they do fit," CC said. She was not a fan of loud and bright colors, but such colors constituted Anne's wardrobe.

"It's like they were made for me. Anyway. . ." Anne pulled the spoon out of her large orange Prada bag. She had wrapped it very carefully in a white cotton handkerchief. She handed it to CC. "Look at the mark on the back. In all my years of collecting spoons, I've never seen a mark like that before!"

"Interesting." CC turned the spoon over in her hand. "Looks like the letter *P*."

"Can we use your computer and look it up?"

"Sure." They walked into the house and sat in front of CC's 23-inch iMac. Opening the search engine, CC typed *silver marks* into the search field. Immediately, images of silver marks came up. Anne leaned closer over CC's shoulder to see the results.

CC scrolled through the long list of images and compared them to the one on the back of the spoon, which she was still holding. "I'm not seeing it. Nothing looks like the mark on this spoon."

"Me neither." Anne released a large sigh. "I don't even know where to start looking from here."

"I don't either," said CC. "Maybe at the auction house when they have their free appraisals?"

"I don't want to sell it!" Anne grabbed the spoon back from CC.

CC stood up from the computer. "I'll make us some tea and we can figure out where to go from here."

CC's house was in direct contrast to Anne's cluttered bungalow. It was neat, organized and efficient, as was CC— thanks to her German upbringing. She came back to the living room with a Rogers' silver service that she'd picked up at an estate sale, a bargain for only $25. Anne took a sugar cube from the bowl with the silver tongs, thought about it and then took two more. CC watched with a disapproving eye. She was not a fan of excess of any kind.

"So, we know what the spoon isn't. Now we have to figure out what it is. That should narrow it down a little. The problem is getting a clearer view of the mark."

"I wonder if I could use my microscope at work," Anne said.

Chapter Twenty-Four

Usually Anne wasn't very excited to go to work but on Monday she was early for the first time in many years. She couldn't examine the spoon first thing because there was actual work to do. Throughout the day, she kept looking at her purse, the spoon calling out to her. She just had to make it to lunch and then she could start her investigation. When the clock ticked noon, she ran to her purse. The rest of the chemists and lab technicians were either at lunch or in the cafeteria. Anne stayed behind. Placing the spoon under the microscope she could zoom in on the mark. However, the mark was too worn to even make out under the microscope.

She sent CC a quick text to tell her she couldn't make out the mark. CC was on deadline and probably wouldn't be checking her phone regularly. Perhaps she could find the answer in a book. Anne stopped on her way home at her favorite used bookstore. She still liked the weight and feel of paper versus the cold click of a computer keyboard. For someone who'd worked in technology all day, she rarely used it after hours. She hated the inhumanity of it. Besides, she loved walking up and down the aisles.

By the time she got home, Sassy was furious. It was an hour and half past dinnertime. This was unacceptable. Sassy relayed her feelings to Anne by not doing her usual purr and wrap around her ankles. Sassy would teach her a lesson.

"Sorry, Sass, I know I'm running a little late." Dropping her bagful of books, Anne bent down to pet the Persian who was oblivious until the can opener sounded. Then all that was wrong was right.

Anne made herself a turkey wrap and grabbed a diet ginger ale. Before settling into her favorite chair by the fireplace, she stopped to admire the stained glass fire screen she'd picked up on one of her excursions. It was difficult for her to hold her attention on the glass when so many things were calling to her from around the room. Strengthening her resolve, she opened one of her new old books. She had a lot of research to do. At 9:03 p.m., her phone rang. It was CC. She'd finally received Anne's text and was anxious to hear more about the spoon.

"I stopped at Secondhand Books, and bought every book I could on silversmithing," Anne said.

"Why didn't you just go to the library?"

"I can't use my library card. I owe them money." Anne paused. "Oh, I forgot to tell you what happened when we were at the Highland Park sale."

"Is it about the pants?" CC asked.

"No, though those pants are fantastic." Anne paused again. "I overheard a conversation between Mr. Ripley and some man named Banning about Tim Whitmore's nephew being upset about a spoon."

"Do you think they're talking about your spoon?"

"There were several silver settings for sale there—in much better condition than mine. I can't imagine he would be upset about an old tarnished teaspoon that doesn't even belong to a set."

"Are you going to contact Mr. Ripley?"

"No, it's mine now. I paid for it, and I'm keeping it."

"If what you're saying is true, the only one who seems to know anything about the spoon is Whitmore's nephew," CC said. "Don't you think he has a right to know what happened to it?"

Anne struggled. It was a moral dilemma of biblical proportions. On one hand, she'd paid fair and square; on the other hand, she supposed he did have a right to know where it had ended up. Besides, he might have more of his uncle's antiques which hadn't been sold at the estate sale, and Anne was never opposed to taking a road trip for antiques. Dilemma solved. "Okay, CC."

CC went to her iMac and Googled *Tim Whitmore*. It brought up his obituary. "It says here he was originally from Moreland, Illinois," she read to Anne.

Anne interrupted, "Where's Moreland?"

"Let me finish," CC continued reading, "He is survived by his nephew Jared Whitmore. There's no phone number or address for Jared. Let me look up Moreland."

She Googled *Morelan*d. "Anne, Moreland is off of Route 125 downstate. That's where the Lincoln Yard Sale is Fourth of July weekend. We've talked for years about going to that sale." CC Googled Lincoln Homestead Yard Sale and found a website that detailed the route of the weekend-long sale, which extended from various areas where Lincoln had settled before he became president. "We could wind up in Springfield for the fair."

Road trip! Anne's eyes lit up. Normally, Anne wasn't a large fan of garage sales. She felt they were mostly used to offload baby toys and clothes that nobody would ever wear. But maybe this sale would be different.

They made arrangements to leave early in the morning. After hanging up from Anne, CC went to the *Chicago Tribune* website. There she saw her picture—front and center with Anne and the pants! CC skimmed the article and at the bottom saw the link to her blog,

"Oh, good; they put our blog site on there." She clicked over to her blog and saw there had now been over 12,000 views. New comments were noted at 2,200. She ran downstairs and grabbed the bottle of Asti she'd been saving. She skipped back into the living room with Bandit skipping around her. "Booboo Bear, this is good, very, very good!" She popped open the sparkling wine and drank it right from the bottle. Bandit took care of everything that spilled on the oak floor.

She sat down to scroll through the comments. Many were from readers sharing their own experiences with antiques, but the majority were from people looking for stuff. She grabbed her reporter's notebook from her bag and added the new items to her list. She probably should start cataloging them by type such as household, tools, and games. Maybe she and Anne could find some things this weekend during their road trip.

Chapter Twenty-Five

They took the car less likely to break down—CC's red Pontiac Grand Am. In the passenger seat, Anne played navigator and was guiding them according to the turn-by-turn directions on Google maps. She couldn't stand the robotic voice so she preferred to read along as they drove. She leaned back for a long ride as the suburban landscape gave way to rows and rows of early summer corn. While the upper third of Illinois was urban, this part of central Illinois was all farmland and native prairie.

"Hey, CC," Anne said as she looked through an Illinois guidebook of unusual sights. "It says here this guy in Gilman created a rock garden to memorialize his wife. We should stop. It says visitors are welcome. A rock garden could be neat. . ."

CC interrupted her, "Anne, we're barely going to get there as it is. Plus, I think Gilman is completely in the other direction."

Anne sighed. She relished every chance to get out of her suburban comfort zone. She liked visiting far away places. She never knew what treasures awaited her there. "There's an Amish enclave in Arthur," she read.

"Anne," CC said, frustrated. CC was more pragmatic and liked to focus on the task at hand.

They drove along. About 30 miles outside of Springfield, they started seeing signs for the "Lincoln Yard Sale," the second longest yard sale in the Midwest. The thought of miles and miles of bargains was almost too much for Anne to stand. Fifteen miles outside of Springfield, traffic slowed down; five miles out of Springfield it was at a dead stop. They bypassed Springfield proper and headed down the back roads.

"I think the real finds are off the beaten path," Anne said.

CC pulled her vintage Ray Ban Wayfarers down to the tip of her nose and looked over the top as the overhung oaks, elms and maples made a canopy of shade. There was something romantic about back roads. CC thought about Tony. She hadn't allowed herself that pleasure since seeing his wedding ring the other day, but she thought how nice it would be to be traveling a back road like this one with him.

"Stop!" Anne screamed.

CC slammed on the brakes. "What? What's wrong?"

"Look!" she said, pointing at the first house which popped up through the poplars. It was a well-worn farmhouse set back from the road; the yard was covered with long tables. From her perch on the passenger seat, Anne couldn't see what was on the tables but she knew she had to look. CC pulled over halfway into the drainage ditch on the side of the road.

The girls exited the car, Anne moving quicker than CC.

There were hand-drawn colorful cardboard signs with Abraham Lincoln's picture and *Yard Sale* written all over them. The first table was littered with piles and piles of clothes—ranging from children's to adult sizes, many still bearing Wal-Mart tags. They nodded hello to the harried-looking woman sitting on a lawn chair wearing her Wal-Mart best. A battle was being waged between the woman and the chair. For now, she was winning, but the chair was crying uncle.

Three young boys buzzed around her like fireflies, except these she didn't swat. She just screamed at them to settle down. The young boys had their mother's red hair and freckles. They also had the devil's energy. CC thought about what it'd be like to be in that house at bedtime and a cold shiver went down her spine. It made her glad that she'd never had kids.

The woman sipped her ice tea. "You ladies lookin' for something in particular? We got everything."

"You're our first stop," Anne said.

The Wal-Mart lady said, "You don't want to regret not buying something when you see it. Things go fast during the Lincoln Yard Sale. Last year, I was sold out after two days."

CC noticed an old Ford tractor peeking out from behind the house. "Excuse me, I noticed your tractor back there. Is that an 9N?"

"You got a good eye. It sure is. That's my grandfather's 1940 Ford. Is that the kind of thing you're looking for?"

"I like any farm or industrial tools."

"We haven't farmed this land since my grandfather passed. There's some stuff in the barn that you might be interested in." The Wal-Mart lady struggled to get out of the lawn chair. The legs bowed and creaked as she was finally released from its hold. The waffle tattoo on the back of her thighs was the lawn chair's revenge.

CC followed her to the barn, watching the tattoo disappear and her breathing get louder. When she reached the barn door, the Wal-Mart lady turned and said, "The roof's a little leaky, so be careful."

She opened the door, and it gave a loud creak. She brushed away the cobwebs. The sunlight rushed into the barn, highlighting the rusty traps hanging from the ceiling. The walls were lined with pitchforks, rakes, milk pails, shovels, and bales of barbed wire. Engine parts and tires lined one side of the barn. CC stepped carefully, avoiding the raccoon droppings. She could feel a thousand beady red eyes looking at her from dark corners of the barn. "How old is that barbed wire?" CC asked, pointing. She walked over to examine it more closely.

"That was here when my grandfather was a little boy. It's been here as far back as I can remember. We never strung any barbed wire, but my grandfather wasn't one for throwing anything away," The Wal-Mart lady said.

CC recognized the pattern of the wire as an early example of Lucien B. Smith's work, which was very collectible. Dating back to 1886, Smith was the first to patent barbed wire. "Is this something you'd consider selling?" CC asked the woman.

She did not hesitate. "What do you think it's worth?"

CC paused. "It's been sitting here under the raccoon poop for how many decades? It's not something you're going to use. I have to tell you that it's worth money to the right collector." CC could never take advantage of someone who didn't know what they had. "I'd give you a hundred for the one bale," CC said.

The Wal-Mart lady appeared quite pleased with the number. CC ran back to the car to get her wallet and her leather workman's gloves that she always carried.

While CC was in the barn, Anne perused the tables, thoughtfully picking up various items and then setting them back down. Her eyes settled on a water-stained cardboard box. Opening it, she found a collection of daguerreotypes. These early photographs were composed on a mirror-like surface of silver and reflected back either light or dark, depending on the process. An early example of photography, these late 1800s images were very collectible and one of the items on their list. The masking tape price tag said *$35.*

CC and the Wal-Mart lady returned from the barn, CC carefully carrying the barbed wire. "Anne, I'm going to put this in the trunk," she called over.

"Okay," Anne said, waving her off, holding the cardboard box in her hands. "Hi, I'm interested in this box," Anne said to the Wal-Mart lady who'd settled back in the lawn chair.

"What do I have that marked?" The lady peered at the tag.

"Would you be willing to take $20?" Anne asked.

"Those are real old. They've been in my family a long time. I got to get at least $30 for them."

"Okay," Anne quickly agreed. She opened up her wallet and handed the woman the money. "Do you have anything I can wrap these in? We have a long drive."

The woman handed Anne some napkins and Wal-Mart bags. Anne very carefully wrapped each photographic image in the napkins and the bags before putting them back in the box. "Thank you," she said, walking to the car where CC was waiting.

"What'd you find?" CC asked after Anne had settled back in the passenger seat. She'd gently placed the box on the floor of the back seat.

"I found a box of daguerreotypes. A box of ten of them. I think one or two might be African American images. I can sell each one on eBay for a few hundred dollars, and I only paid $30 for the whole box," Anne said. "And, they are one of the items on our list."

The next several houses they drove past because they had baby clothes, children's toys and rusty bicycles—nothing on their list and nothing they'd be interested in. Throughout the day, they stopped at various houses, picking up different items including a McCoy planter, a wooden barn birdhouse, a case of green mason jars, spools and a silk scarf, checking off items as they went along.

"This is so exciting. All these people depending on us to make their dreams come true," Anne said, reviewing the pages and pages of CC's cramped handwriting on the list.

"I don't know if it's that dramatic."

"Think about it. Think about how you felt when you found your dining room set. How'd you feel?"

"I felt good. It was exactly what I wanted. I was happy to get it."

"Exactly. The harder it is to find, the sweeter the reward," Anne said. "Right? How many times do you just sit and stare at your 1920s slag glass lamp? How do you feel when you read one of your biographies?"

"I feel good. I feel connected to it. It's special."

"Exactly. Just like you and me. We're unique."

"Yes, Anne, we are unique."

"I could see us making a living out of this. We quit our jobs—do this full time. Travel the country just like those guys on that show you like to watch. Except prettier."

CC laughed. "Yes, prettier."

"Stop, stop, pull over!" Anne shouted. On the edge of a cornfield, there was a tractor with a sign on the side saying *Barn Sale*. "Yes, *Barn Sale;* two of my favorite words."

The gravel kicked up under CC's Grand Am as she spun down the winding road leading to a red barn with a large American flag painted on its side. Several cars were parked out in front along with a farmer who was parked behind a folding table.

The outside was cluttered with milk pails, concrete lawn animals, hand-held farm tools and corn-stalk scarecrows. Anne got out of the car and picked up a scarecrow with a straw hat. "This is really charming."

Inside were copper cowbell wind chimes that clanked in the afternoon breeze. A pile of old almanacs were clustered on a wooden table. CC thumbed through them. They dated back to the 1860s and were in excellent condition. She piled them up in her arm. Anne came along, dragging a butter churn and milk pail. They stopped and looked at each other. "How are we going to fit all this in the car?"

"We can ship it home."

"That's crazy. We're going to spend more in shipping than this stuff is worth."

"We can pay for it and then come back later."

"I'm not driving another 12 hours back here."

They brought their items out to the farmer and asked him to hold them while they continued to look. "CC, come here!" Anne was waving madly from a table near the barn entrance.

CC walked over.

"I think these are authentic. I think it's John Zadzora." Anne held up a winged wall packet that appeared to have been hand carved.

"He was a famous tramp artist," CC said, taking the piece from Anne and examining it. "You know *tramp* comes from the German *trampen*, which acknowledged the craftsmen's' apprenticeship in medieval times. It came into its own in the 1850s when cigars became popular. Artists would use their cigar boxes to carve various items using a pocketknife."

"Yes, I know all that," Anne interrupted her. "I think this is one of the items on our list."

CC pulled the list out of her purse and scanned it. "Yes, it is. Let's add it to our pile," she said, taking the piece outside and to the farmer. They split up again and walked around the overfilled barn, picking up occasional pieces here and there. Anne's pile was growing with additional finds including an early copy of *The Wizard of Oz* complete with the original illustrations, a pink Fostoria vase and some children's wooden spinning tops. This was the best stop of the day. As she carried items out to the table, she could tell the farmer thought so, too.

As the hours passed away, the sun shifted over to the American flag side of the barn and the sunlight came sifting in. That's when CC saw it. Just a glimpse of the big VW illuminated by the afternoon light. It was rusty, the windows were broken, and all the tires were flat, but CC had never seen anything so beautiful. It was a 1968 Volkswagen microbus. It was the same model year that CC's father had driven in Germany right before they moved to America. She threw open the sliding door of the van which didn't give lightly and groaned with a metal on metal cry. The inside was in pretty good shape or at least the mice thought so as they scurried out. She climbed in and sat in the driver's seat, caressing the leather-wrapped steering wheel. She imagined driving down the open road—no deadlines, no editors, and no problems. Anne poked her head in the passenger window. "This thing is huge inside. We could fit everything in here."

"That's not going to happen now. It's going to need a lot of restoration," CC said.

"Yeah, but it's going to be awesome when we're done, isn't it?"

CC nodded, still staring out the windshield, turning the steering wheel like she was already on the road.

The farmer walked up to them. "Barn sale's over. It's almost five. You're the last ones. I got to lock up," he said.

"Is the bus for sale?" CC asked, getting out of the van.

"I got plans to restore her. I got some extra parts in the back of the barn." He hooked his thumbs threw his overalls.

"How long have you owned it?"

"About 20 years."

"After having it sit like this for 20 years, you still plan on fixing it up?"

"I guess you have a point. I'd consider an offer if the number was right."

CC pulled out her iPhone and went to *oldbug.com*. There were mint restored 1968 microbuses going for $16,000. She'd taken several shop classes at the College of DuPage after her divorce and had actually become a pretty fair shade tree mechanic. She had the tools and she could read a repair manual as good as the next fellow. "I'll give you $2,000," she said.

The farmer thought for a second and smiled. "The parts are worth more than that. I can part it out and get $3,500."

"What about this? We've got all the stuff we piled up at your table. We got the butter churn, the milk pail, some old folk arty things, and the almanacs. What if we give you $3,000 for everything?" Anne said.

"I can do that," the farmer said, shaking both their hands.

The girls paid him and made arrangements to have the van picked up. They took what they could carry in the car and left the rest in the van.

Leaving the barn sale, they followed the yard sale signs into Champaign, home of the University of Illinois. "Let's have dinner," CC said, knowing they'd find something decent around the campus and that most of the sales would be closing by now.

"One more sale?" Anne asked, giving CC a hopeful look.

They drove through the university campus, admiring the historic buildings, which ran right through the town. The whole town was built around the university.

"I'm starving. Let's stop and get something to eat before Moreland," CC said.

"Just one more sale, please, and then we can eat," Anne said.

"How about that one right there?" CC pointed to a two-story brick Georgian. Its front lawn had tables of household wares and what appeared to be boxes of books. She pulled the car over.

Anne ran out and walked over to the tables. CC rifled through the boxes, checking out all the history books. There were a lot of textbooks, biographies, and all things that she enjoyed reading. She started a pile. As she was looking, a white-haired petite woman wearing a cotton sundress walked up to her. "Hello," the woman said. "Can I help you find anything?"

"I'd like to take it all. You have such a great collection of books," CC said, holding a large stack in her arms.

"I can't take credit for that. Those are mostly my husband's. He's retired now. He taught history at the university. Hold on." She walked to the house and came back out carrying a book. "This is his." She flipped the book to reveal a political tome. "This is one of the ones he wrote on pre-1850s American history."

CC took the book out of her hand, and read the flyleaf. "This is really interesting. I'd love to buy a copy."

"Of course."

"Do you think he would sign it for me?"

"Of course. He's in his study. Why don't you come in the house? I'm sure he'd love to meet you."

CC followed her up the concrete steps into the house. "Daniel, this young lady would like you to sign one of your books," the woman called out.

A distinguished looking man with a shock of unruly white hair came out of a room off the front of the house. He walked with a bit of a shuffle and a little bit of a shake. He gave a big warm smile. He grabbed CC's hand in both of his. "So nice to meet you. I'm Professor Elliott. I see you have my book on American history."

"Yes, I'm fascinated by early American history," CC said.

Mrs. Elliott came back in the door with Anne. Professor Elliott took a fountain pen out of his shirt pocket. "What would you like me to write?"

"Just say, 'To CC Muller'."

As he signed it, he asked, "Are you from the area?"

"No, we came down from Chicago for the yard sale."

"Chicago. I love Chicago. I have many friends up there."

"We're on our way to Moreland to find out some information about an antique we picked up at an estate sale," CC said.

"Yes, a spoon," Anne said. She ran out of the house to the car. Moments later, she came back in and unwrapped the spoon from its cotton handkerchief.

Professor Elliott took his glasses from around his neck and put them on his nose to get a better look. "Very interesting." He turned the spoon over in his hand to get a closer look at the signature. "Can we go into my study? I have my loupe there," the professor said, leading the way into a book-lined room. The walls were covered floor to ceiling with dark wood bookcases lined with books. An elaborate wood fireplace stood out on one wall. An oak desk was at the far end near a bay window. Behind the desk, was a red leather desk chair. The girls sat in the chairs across from his desk. He pulled a loupe out of his draw, holding it to his eye, as he examined the back of the spoon. "Incredible," he murmured. "This looks like a Paul Revere die stamp. The bottom of the *R* is faded."

"I'm familiar with Paul Revere's work, and I've never seen any spoon of his that looked like this. Most of his pieces are very utilitarian," CC said. "He wasn't very skilled at scrollwork or engraving."

"From what I know, you are correct. Most of his spoons are very simple, but this is definitely his hallmark. Of course, you need a more knowledgeable expert to verify if this is an authentic Paul Revere." The professor handed the spoon back to Anne.

She looked closer at what she thought was a *P* on the back of the spoon. "CC, it's an *R*. The bottom part is worn off. That is definitely an *R*. I can see it now."

"I know someone." He reached into his drawer and pulled out a card. "Wayne Muscarello; he's a colleague at the University of Chicago who'd know more about this."

Anne interrupted. "I know Wayne."

"He also works at the Field Museum, and he'd be able to confirm if this is a Paul Revere spoon. We've collaborated on some of my books on the Revolution. He'd be the one to verify if this is authentic or not." The professor handed them a business card.

Anne took the card. "Thank you so much, Professor. We will visit him when we get back to Chicago."

Anne and CC thanked the professor and paid for their books. Both still in shock, neither one of them said a word as they walked back to the car.

They ate at a small diner across from the campus. Anne ate with one hand, clutching her purse, the spoon safely hidden inside. "CC, what do we do now? CC, what if this is a Paul Revere spoon? Should I even be carrying this around?"

"Let's start with Whitmore's nephew first," CC said.

Anne nodded in agreement. She was terrified it would be a fake but even more terrified that it was real.

After their dinner, they drove the approximately 45-minute drive to Moreland. Moreland was one of those towns that was a mere dot on the map. One of those towns where if you blinked, you'd miss it.

While only 216 miles from Chicago, it was a hundred years away. The town boasted of a one-mile long main strip. Most of the shops were closed, but Anne was delighted to see one antique store. She strained to look in its windows as they drove past.

They arrived at the old-fashioned Moreland Inn. After checking them in at the front desk, CC drove the car to the parking space directly in front of their room.

They walked into the room, lugging Anne's monstrous suitcase to find twin beds and not much else. It looked like the room hadn't been decorated since the 1970s. CC turned to Anne and said, "It's just a place to sleep. We're not going to be in the room that much."

Anne sighed and sat down on the springy mattress.

Chapter Twenty-Six

After a good night's sleep, they walked over to the adjoining coffee shop, The Moreland Grind. Anne had changed into the flowered pants. "Did you bring any other clothes or is this your new thing?" CC asked.

"These pants are so comfortable."

The two walked into the coffee shop where they were greeted by MaryAnne, the waitress, a woman in her 60s who apparently ate a lot of free pie. She was holding a pot of coffee and some napkins. "Morning, ladies, would you like a table or a booth?"

"Booth is fine," Anne said.

"I like your pants," MaryAnne said, brushing past them, heading towards a booth.

"Hmmp," CC said as they walked over to the booth and settled in.

MaryAnne fluttered around the tables. *For a large woman, she was quite graceful*, CC thought. "I think our first stop should be public records or the courthouse so we can track down Jared Whitmore," CC said. "We can look at public tax records. Maybe stop at the local newspaper and see if there are any articles. Here, I've made up a list." CC pulled a reporter's notebook out of her purse.

MaryAnne came up to the table as CC was continuing. "I have another idea," Anne said, turning to MaryAnne. "MaryAnne, we're looking for Jared Whitmore."

"Are you friends or family?" MaryAnne said.

"We knew his uncle."

"What a shame. You know, Tim grew up here. I actually went to high school with him," MaryAnne said. "He was kind of goofy but nice. You know, once he moved to Chicago we didn't see him much. He was never quite the same after winning the Powerball." She paused. "Jared has a place about six miles south of town off of 19."

"Great, MaryAnne, thank you."

"Would you like to order now?" MaryAnne said.

After their breakfast arrived, CC pulled a tiny glass jar out of her purse. She sprinkled the hot peppery mix on her scrambled eggs. Noticing Anne's look, CC said, "It makes everything better."

"I don't know how you can eat that," Anne said. "My eyes are watering over here just smelling it."

While CC finished her coffee, Anne looked through the classifieds in the local paper. "CC, there's not much going on here, but there is one thing that sounds interesting."

"Anne, let's keep to the plan." CC finished her coffee, and they headed down 19, a two-lane highway. As they were driving, they spotted a mailbox on the side of a gravel road. Sticking her head out the window, Anne made out the name *Whitmore* on the mailbox. CC turned down the gravel road that disappeared into the woods. It was a much less pleasant winding road than the one they'd driven to the other Whitmore house. CC had a feeling that Jared Whitmore's house wasn't as pleasant either.

The first *Do Not Enter* sign popped up as they turned a corner. It was full of bullet holes. "Anne, I think this might not be a good idea," CC said, looking at Anne, who was staring out the window.

The second *Do Not Enter* sign was crudely made and larger than the first. "I'm getting the impression that we might not be welcome," CC said, stopping the car.

"We can't stop now. We've come this far," Anne said.

CC continued on. When they reached the end of the gravel road, they came upon a rundown farmhouse. It wasn't much to look at. Its whitewash had faded to gray, its black shutters dangled off their hinges, the windows were broken in places, and the screen door smiled a toothless grin. They pulled up and got out of the car. They walked up the wooden stairs and looked through the hole in the screen door. "See; the door's open," Anne said.

"Are you crazy?" CC asked. "I don't feel good about this." She gazed around, waving off the buzzing flies.

Anne walked over to the porch window and put her face up to the window, shading the sun with her hands. Anne swatted at the flies buzzing around her face. "I don't see anyone," she said.

A clatter of metal sounded from somewhere behind them. They rushed back down the porch. CC started towards the car and Anne walked towards the noise. In a hushed voice, CC said, "C'mon, what are you doing? We need to get out of here."

"I just want to take a look." Anne crept slowly around the corner of the house, making herself appear as small as possible.

CC sighed and followed her around the back of the house. About 50 yards into the woods, they saw a little shack with smoke rising up out of it. They heard the rattle of metal pans. "They're probably just cooking dinner," Anne said.

"Why would you be cooking in a shack behind the house, not in the house?" CC said, stopping in her tracks.

Anne walked into a beer can trip wire sounding an alarm. A young man with shaggy blonde hair, wearing a torn sleeveless shirt came rushing out of the shed, brandishing a shotgun in his heavily tattooed arms. The girls froze, CC clutching Anne.

"What are you doing here? Who are you?" the man asked, pointing the shotgun at them.

"We knew your uncle. We're here to talk to you about him," CC said.

Jared lowered the shotgun, eyeballing the women. "You knew my uncle, Tim, did you?"

"We didn't know him personally but we were at his estate sale. We're trying to identify one of the items we bought," CC said, nudging Anne. Anne slowly reached into her purse and brought the spoon out.

Jared rested the shotgun against the shack and took the spoon. He looked it over and handed it back. "Never seen it before. Why's it so important?"

"We overheard the estate sale manager talking to some man named Banning. He said that you were asking about it," Anne said.

Jared stopped and thought. "Oh, Banning, he's my uncle's antique dealer. He bought and sold a lot of stuff for him."

"What kind of stuff?" Anne asked.

"You know—antiques—that crap he had all over his house. Banning advised him and purchased things for him."

"Your uncle had a very extensive collection," CC said.

"Uncle Tim didn't know anything about collecting," Jared said, rubbing his jaw, spitting into the red clay and looking angry. "Banning told him what to buy. Cost Uncle Tim a fortune, all he left me was an old gun."

"I thought your uncle won millions from the Powerball. Where'd it all go?" Anne asked.

"Wish I knew," Jared said.

"What about the house and his collection? We were at the estate sale and saw everything he had," Anne said.

"Uncle Tim left a lot of debt. He liked to gamble, and he liked to buy fancy junk. He was trying to fit in with those North Shore snobs," Jared said. "He was ashamed of where he came from."

"Let me take a look at the gun," CC said. Anne grabbed the spoon back out of his hand.

"Follow me." He walked into the farmhouse. CC and Anne followed him in. Looking around, it was obvious he didn't have his uncle's eye for quality. Jared came back to the dark wood-paneled living room holding a long rifle.

CC took it out of his hands and inspected it with a knowing eye. "This is a Massachusetts Minuteman Rifle. It looks authentic."

"Is it worth anything?" Jared asked.

"Depending on who owned it, it could be worth a lot of money," CC said.

Jared took back the rifle. "It's useless. There's something wrong with the barrel. Doesn't matter much. My uncle only shot blanks out of it anyway."

"Why would he shoot blanks?" Anne asked, sitting on the arm of a tattered pink couch.

"Uncle Tim was into reenacting. You know, battles––especially Revolutionary War battles. He and his buddies would go out, dress up and play soldier," Jared said. "I didn't much care for it. I went with him a couple times."

"Can I take the gun?" CC asked, pulling her business card out of her pocket. "I'd be glad to help you sell it. I've seen others in much worse condition sell for thousands of dollars." CC turned the gun over, looking under the barrel.

Jared managed a bit of a smile. "Now, that's what I want to hear." He took a long look at them. He stared at CC's business card and appeared deep in thought. "What does *antique hunters* mean?"

"We connect people with treasures from the past, their childhood memories," Anne said. "If they're looking for it, we can find it."

Cradling the rifle, CC interrupted Anne, "Do you have any mineral oil? Or anything that I can use to clean the rifle?"

"I got some dish soap," Jared said.

"That'll work."

Jared came back from the kitchen carrying a bottle of dish soap. CC took a paper towel, moistened it and added a little soap. The dissected snake engraving on the barrel came alive, and she could make out the words *Join or Die*.

She said, "Anne, take a look."

Anne brought her loupe up to her eye and examined the image. CC looked up at Jared with a smile on her face. "Sons of Liberty," Anne said, getting excited.

Jared gave Anne and CC a blank stare. CC gave him a history lesson and said, "The Sons of Liberty were mostly local shopkeepers and tradesmen in Boston before the Revolutionary war. Sam Adams, Paul Revere, Patrick Henry and John Hancock were all members. This is their emblem."

Jared continued to look confused. "You know about the Boston Tea Party?" CC said. "The Sons of Liberty planned and executed the Boston Tea Party to protest the Stamp Act. They met at the Green Dragon Tavern to plan their revolt. I visited the tavern when I was there once for a conference in Boston."

"Is that so?" He scratched at the stubble on his chin. "You might want to talk to the guys that Uncle Tim played soldier with. They might be interested in buying the gun. They have a reenactment every Fourth of July in Springfield," Jared said.

"Thank you, I'll contact you once I find out more about your gun," CC said, jotting down Jared's phone number.

They walked outside and stood by their car on the gravel road. "Hold up a second," Jared said, running toward the shack. He came back, carrying a Mason jar. "Here's a little something for the road."

Not wanting to insult him, CC took the jar. "Thank you." She threw the jar in the back seat and drove off.

The two friends left Jared and headed back north toward Chicago. "Hey, look, we're going to be driving right past Springfield," Anne said, reading from one of her guidebooks. "It's the state fair weekend. There's a Revolutionary War reenactment that Jared mentioned. Let's stop and find someone who knew Tim Whitmore. Maybe they can give us some answers about Tim and the spoon." Anne paused. "Speaking of Jared." She reached behind the passenger seat and picked up the Mason jar. "What are we going to do with this?" She unclasped the Mason jar and a foul odor immediately filled the car. Her eyes watered and her nostrils flared.

CC looked over with a horrified expression. "Close it!"

Anne panicked and dropped the Mason jar spilling it all over the car, causing CC to swerve into oncoming traffic. She pulled the car back hard to the right, overcompensating and running onto the shoulder, a split second before nearly driving head on into a semi-, whose horn was still blaring.

By the time she'd regained control of the car, a Springfield police officer was on her tail. The tilt-awhirl police light filled her rear view mirror and the siren drowned out Anne's screaming. CC pulled the car over to the shoulder, trying to figure out how to explain smelling like a hundred proof moonshine. And, she had to explain the rifle sitting up in the backseat.

Anne took out her lace handkerchief and desperately tried to dab away the moonshine smell. CC looked at her and said, "Really?"

The trooper tapped on the driver's window. CC rolled it down. Both girls turned to the left with their biggest smiles. Anne stopped dabbing up the moonshine.

The trooper took a sniff. "Please exit the car, ma'am."

"Officer, it's not what you think," CC said, reaching for the door handle.

"Ma'am, please exit the car," the trooper repeated. Anne reached for her door handle. "Not you, ma'am. Just the driver." CC got out of the car slowly.

The trooper took a step back and said something into the two-way radio clipped to his shoulder. "Ma'am, have you been drinking?"

"Officer, I have not. By mistake, there was a mason jar in the car. We didn't know it had moonshine in it and it spilled," CC said.

"Ma'am, moonshine is illegal in Illinois unless it's stamped from a licensed distillery," he said. "Any open alcohol in a vehicle is against the law. I need to see your driver's license, proof of insurance and registration."

CC had everything in her hand already and gave it to him.

"Ma'am, I need you to take a Breathalyzer test."

"I realize you have probable cause. I've not been drinking, and I don't want to take a Breathalyzer test.

Statistics show that eight percent of breathalyzers are inconclusive or even worse false positives," CC said.

The trooper called in CC's information. "Ma'am, were you aware that you have three outstanding red light tickets?"

She hemmed. "I did receive some notices but I feel that they're unconstitutional. Did you know there is a five percent variable error for red light cameras? It's true. Google it."

"Ma'am, I'm going to have to take you into the station." By the time they were done talking, a second and third police car pulled in behind them. A tow truck followed the two cars. Anne and CC sat in the back of the trooper car, listening to the squawk of the police radio. Anne was taking deep breaths, counting to ten. It wasn't working.

CC was trying to think who to call. It was after 5 p.m., on a Friday night when they arrived at the Springfield police station. CC was afraid they'd have to wait until Monday for a hearing. The officer brought them in front of the desk sergeant.

"I'd like to make my one phone call," Anne said.

"Actually, you're not limited to one. We haven't charged you with anything yet," the sergeant said.

Anne sat on the bench as the sergeant discussed the situation with the arresting officer and CC who was brandishing her press credentials. She kept dropping the governor's name. She had interviewed him for an article a while back. The desk sergeant was not impressed.

"Hello, Nigel," Anne whispered into the phone, cupping the phone with her hand so nobody could hear her.

"Hi, Anne. Are you back from your trip?" Nigel asked.

"I'm in the Springfield police station."

"Is that part of your trip?" he said with his charming, dry wit.

"It's kind of a funny story." Anne explained about Jared, the moonshine and their police escort into town. "Can you talk to somebody here? Can you help us out?"

"Springfield, yes. I'll talk to the captain there and see if I can do anything."

"Thank you, Nigel; thank you so much." Anne paused. "Have you found Jack?" she asked.

Anne could hear the worry in his silence. "The St. Paul police are looking for him. His parents haven't seen him. We'll find him."

"Thank you again."

Anne hung up feeling a little better about the situation. When she walked back over to the sergeant's desk, CC and the sergeant were laughing. Not the reaction that Anne was expecting. "Anne, come here and meet Sergeant Pat. His wife is one of our fans."

"One of our fans? She reads the blog?" Anne asked.

"She read the article about the bear and she was hooked after that. She reads it all the time. She's going to want to meet you two," the sergeant said. "I'll tell you what, as far as the charges, the first offense for possession of moonshine is a misdemeanor. It has a fine. I can tell by talking to you that you're not drunk. As far as the red light tickets, if you promise to pay them and everything else checks out, we can let you go with a warning." He paused. "You can do me a favor." He waved them over to come closer to his desk and they leaned in as he talked in a soft voice, "My anniversary's coming up. My wife's always wanted an antique cameo locket—a genuine hand-carved one. Can you find one for me?"

"We will," Anne said. "I have one in mind already. We'd be glad to do that for you, yes, sir."

He handed them his card and waved over the arresting officer. He explained the situation and the jailbirds were free.

Chapter Twenty-Seven

With the state fair in town, all the hotels were filled. Using her guidebook, Anne found a small bed and breakfast not too far from the fairgrounds. Luckily, they had one small room left. It was an attic room with a separate bathroom. The original wood floors creaked under their feet with every step. Civil war-era paintings hung on the wall depicting a young Lincoln. A homemade quilt decorated the bed. There was a cozy rocking chair in the corner that overlooked the rose garden.

CC flopped onto the feather-down mattress, exhausted. Her shoulders ached from driving.

Anne sat at the cherry wood vanity table. She had not let the spoon out of her sight since they'd met with Professor Elliott. She took it out of her purse and laid it on the table. She thought of what she would do with the money if she could bring herself to sell it. But how could she? Her whole life had been about hunting down pieces of history and here she'd found a piece of the puzzle—a corner piece. She held it in her hand, savoring its weight, picturing herself in Boston Harbor on the tall ship Eleanor. "More sugar, Mr. Adams? Would you like a little milk, Mr. Revere?" she giggled to herself.

From the bed, CC said, "Huh? What did you say? What are you talking about?"

"Nothing; didn't realize I was talking out loud," Anne said.

CC sat up on the edge of the bed. "I'm going to take a shower. Mrs. Hull said dinner is at 6 p.m., sharp. I don't think we should be late. Do you want to change first?"

"I'm fine. I'm going to wear what I have on," Anne said.

CC gave a pointed look at the pants and said, "Hmmph." CC headed for the shower.

Dinner was precisely at six. CC and Anne were on time. The dining room was already filled with fellow guests, there for the Fourth of July festivities. They all nodded and introduced themselves as Mrs. Hull brought in the first course of peanut soup. "Tonight, we'll be dining as our founding fathers would have," she said, placing the soup bowl in the center of the table. "This first course comes to you from Virginia. Peanut soup."

"Yum," Anne said, taking a sip of the steaming soup.

CC reached into her purse to retrieve her pepper jar. Anne touched her knee and whispered to her, " That might be rude to our host."

CC nodded in agreement and let the pepper jar be. The conversation was casual and pleasant. The couple from Minnesota, Stuart and Tracy, seemed to really enjoy the whole Revolutionary War-themed dinner and talked about their outing to the reenactment that they'd gone to during the day. Mrs. Hull brought in a roast beef with homemade biscuits and potatoes. Just when they couldn't eat anymore, Mrs. Hull pushed open the swinging door from the kitchen with her backside and turned around with a silver tray filled with small china bowls of bread pudding.

"I've never had bread pudding before. It's quite good," Tracy said.

"The colonists brought bread pudding from England as a way to use leftover bread. It was known as a poor man's pudding," CC said, taking a breath to continue. Anne nudged her under the table.

"Coffee, anyone?" Mrs. Hull fluttered back into the dining room, walking over to the sideboard, which bore the weight of both a coffee and a tea service in silver.

"None for me," Anne said, looking at her watch.

Chapter Twenty-Eight

The Illinois State Fairgrounds were a beehive of activity. Carnival rides were in full swing and Credence Clearwater Revival filled the air. Cotton candy, corndogs and popcorn assaulted their noses. The smell of fried everything was everywhere. As Anne and CC walked through the carnival, they avoided the hawkers by the midway games. The rock music and rhetoric faded, giving way to the distant call of the fife and drum.

"You know, Anne, the reason they used the fife and drum was because it was the only way for officers to command troops over a distance. The fife was picked because of its high pitch, and the drum because of its low pitch," CC explained as they climbed the slight grassy hill. They could see the bivouacked troops below. The tents billowed in the summer wind. The splash of red of the British troops on one side, the other side adorned with the blue of the Continental Army and the assorted colors of the Minute Men in the militia. On the outskirts of the camp, women stirred vegetables in iron kettles over open fires.

CC and Anne walked toward the Continental Armies' camp. As they walked through the rows of tents, they asked the re-enactors about Tim Whitmore. The troops were assembling; the reenactment of the battle of Lexington was about to begin. A younger officer approached CC. "Excuse me, ma'am; we're going to be starting. You have to clear the field," he said.

CC recognized the Chicago accent. Usually people from Chicago don't admit they have an accent, but CC had a very good ear for dialect, particularly this south side Irish Chicago accent. "Thank you. Are you from Beverly?" she asked, naming a south side Chicago neighborhood which held its own St. Patrick's Day parade every year that was better attended than the downtown Chicago one.

The lieutenant appeared surprised. "How could you tell?"

"I spent a lot of time on the south side. I could hear it in your voice."

"Yes, I am. Born and raised south side Irish." He gave a proud nod.

Maybe you can help us," CC continued. "We're trying to find some information about one of the soldiers from Chicago. Tim Whitmore?"

The lieutenant's face turned sad. "Tim was a good guy. He was in my regiment. He taught me a lot about being a continental soldier. He knew a lot about the battles and took it very seriously. He was the best Paul Revere we ever had."

"Paul Revere?" Anne asked, perking up. She recited the entire Longfellow poem in her head.

"Yes, he would do the whole midnight ride—lantern, horse and all. I was with him in Boston two years ago for the reenactment of the Boston tea party."

With a shaking hand, Anne pulled the spoon from her purse. "Do you remember seeing him with this spoon?"

The lieutenant studied it closely. "Yes, I do. We used it to stir our tea onboard the tall ship in the Boston harbor. I remember it because of its unique design. It was very important for Tim to be accurate. Everything he owned—his uniform, his rifle—were original. No replicas. I suppose this spoon is the real thing too."

Anne took the spoon and wrapped it back in the soft cotton before stowing it away in her purse.

"I was really sorry to hear that he died."

"It's a tragedy," Anne said.

"Ma'am, if you don't mind me asking, why were you asking about the spoon?"

"I bought it at Tim Whitmore's estate sale and wanted to find out more about it," Anne said.

The fife and drum started their call to arms, leaving Anne's words hanging in the air. The lieutenant glanced behind him and noticed his troops gathering for the battle. "I'm sorry. I have to go." He ran off to join the troops who were moving in formation.

The two girls walked off the field and sat on the hill overlooking the battleground. They watched the cannons fire; a second later, the roar rushed over the valley. The drum and fife played as the first soldiers advanced in a line facing their foes—rifles firing and men falling.

Anne caressed the silver spoon the entire time.

After the battle was over, Anne and CC walked back through the crowded midway to find the exit. It seemed like the crowd had doubled since they'd come through. "Look, CC," Anne said, pointing to a directional sign. "They have a flea market here. We should go."

"Anne, we don't have time," CC said, glancing at her watch. It was late Sunday, and they both had to work the next day. "I have to get home to pick Bandit up. He's been with the neighbors all weekend."

Anne trudged behind CC, giving one last longing glance over her shoulder. Next year she'd just drive herself.

Chapter Twenty-Nine

Three hours later, CC pulled into Anne's driveway. It was already 9 p. m., and both travelers were weary. Anne opened the garage door and unloaded all her purchases. The evergreen bush next to the garage shook. Anne jumped back. The tip of the ten-foot evergreen bent over the driveway. "CC!" Anne yelled back to CC who was falling asleep in the car.

CC clicked on the headlights to see yellow eyes piercing out at them from the evergreen. Sassy dropped from the tree like a big white pine cone. "What are you doing out here, Sassy?" Anne said, picking up the indignant Persian. "How'd you get out of the house?" Sassy was in no mood to answer.

From behind the tree, Grandma Jan stepped out. "You got her." Both Anne and CC's hearts stopped for a second. "I heard her crying for the past half hour. I couldn't find her." Grandma Jan was apparently on her nightly rounds, wearing her *Neighborhood Watch* windbreaker and her baseball cap with LED lights that shone brightly from the rim. "Sorry," she said. "Let me turn these off." She reached up to the brim and turned off the lights.

"What's the cat doing outside?" Anne asked.

"I don't know. I heard her crying on my walk and thought maybe you'd let her out by mistake. All the lights were off in your house."

Carrying Sassy, Anne walked up the back stairs. CC and Grandma Jan followed. The door had been kicked in.

"Wait!" Jan said, putting her arm in front of Anne and pulling her back.

She reached into her windbreaker pocket and retrieved a large can of mace. CC immediately called 9-1-1. Anne slowly tiptoed into the kitchen and flipped on the lights. "What are you doing?" CC called out. "Someone could still be in there."

Most visitors wouldn't be able to tell if Anne's house had been ransacked. It looked the way it did everyday, but Anne knew where every piece belonged down to the last napkin ring or thimble. Things were not as they should be, and Anne was not happy. She rushed into the kitchen to make sure her antique coffee grinders were still in place. They were.

"I don't think it's safe to be here," CC said, walking into the kitchen and staring over her friend's shoulder.

Anne grabbed a heavy cast iron skillet. With CC at her heels, they turned on every light in the house and checked every room—even under the beds. Grandma Jan supervised the operation. "Whoever was here is gone now," Anne said, flopping down at the kitchen table.

The doorbell startled Anne and CC. Anne opened the door and was surprised to see Detective Towers who was wearing a tie festooned with pansies. "Miss Hillstrom, we meet again," he said.

"Hi, Nigel, I mean Detective Towers. I wasn't expecting you," Anne said, standing in the doorway.

"I hope you're not disappointed."

"Don't be silly. Apparently you're the only police detective in Chicago," Anne said with a playful smile.

"Your name came up on the call sheet, and I thought it appropriate that I take the call since we have a history."

Nigel's charm and his whimsical ties really worked. She felt more at ease immediately. She'd already forgotten that she was scared. "Please come in," Anne said, opening the door wider.

"Miss Hillstrom, have you touched anything?" he asked, looking around the room.

"Aren't we past last names at this point?" Anne said. "We did have lunch."

Grandma Jan walked into the living room and gave Detective Towers a lookover. "Who is this young man?" she said, circling around the very tall and very British Detective Towers.

"Jan, this is Detective Towers. Detective Towers, this is my neighbor, Jan Kustodia."

"Pleased to meet you, ma'am." Detective Towers bowed his head.

Grandma Jan's concerned look turned to a smile. "British, are you? That's interesting."

"Anne, it is then."

"I just made some tea. We were quite unnerved as you can imagine," Anne said. They all stood in the entryway. "Would you like a cup?"

CC walked into the living room at that moment and was also struck by Nigel's height and mesmerized by his tie. "Detective Towers, nice to meet you. CC Muller." She held out her hand to him. He shook it.

They all walked into the kitchen and sat around the table. "Can I offer you a cup of tea? We still have the tea kettle on," Anne said.

"Tea would be lovely." Nigel sat on a chair, his knees bumping against the table. Anne was reminded of one of her favorite animated Disney movies, *Ichabod Crane and Sleepy Hollow*. "Have you noticed anything missing?" the detective asked, pulling out a small notebook from his coat pocket.

"I've walked around the house and haven't noticed anything off hand. As you can see, there's a lot to look at," Anne said, bringing him a cup of Earl Grey.

The detective scanned the room, which had been restored to its original finish from the black and white tile on the floor to the bead board cabinets. Like the living room, it was cluttered in a cozy way. Assorted teacups hung from wooden pegs over the sink, coffee grinders stood on the shelf, and copper pans sat on the stovetop. "Yes, I can see you have a good eye for antiques. I noticed your poster in the hallway from *Bikini Blood Beach.* That's a very unusual poster," he said. "Not too many people share my love of classic American B movies. It's a passion of mine. I read that costumer Nancy Packwall just died."

Anne did a twirl, showing off the flowered pants. She hadn't taken them off in days. "We went to her estate sale. These are the pants that Stevie Vann wore in the movie and that's where I got the movie poster, too," Anne said.

"The pants are quite lovely," Detective Towers said.

"I'm sorry but I just have to ask," CC interrupted. "The British accent?"

"We came over from Liverpool when I was young."

"How old were you?" CC asked.

"I was about eleven," the detective said.

"That explains it. I just read an article about how children develop their accents by the time they are twelve. That's why you haven't lost it," CC explained.

"CC, back to the break in," Anne said, crossing her arms over her chest.

"I don't understand why someone would break in and not take anything when you have so much to choose from. Can you make a list of anything that's missing?" the detective said. "Do you want me to wait with you?"

"That's okay." Anne hesitated.

"Of course, we want you to wait. Someone just broke into the house," CC said. "I don't even know if it's safe for Anne to stay here tonight."

"Anne, you can stay with me," Grandma Jan interrupted.

Nigel leaned back and sipped his tea. "You should call someone out to fix that lock, but in most cases we find that burglars don't come back," the detective said. "I've not heard of any other recent burglaries in this neighborhood. It seems to be an isolated incident."

They sat while Anne called a few locksmiths. Not wanting to pay the emergency charge, Anne arranged to meet them the next day. Anne walked Nigel out to his car.

"Call me anytime if you can think of anything or find something missing or even if you're just nervous." He took a moment to touch Anne's hand.

Anne held his hand for a moment. "I certainly will, Nigel." Anne was a bit flustered. She'd thought about Nigel since their lunch. She never expected to see him again under these circumstances. She watched him drive away.

CC had been peeking through the living room window. It had been a very long time since she'd seen her friend show any interest in anyone. She could tell by Anne's body language that she was attracted to Nigel. She hid her smile to conceal her snooping.

"Ok, then," Anne said, walking back into the house. "Nigel's on top of this."

"Apparently, he is," CC said with a smirk.

"What's that supposed to mean?" Anne asked.

"Why don't you stay with me?" CC said.

"I think I will," Anne said, and then she turned to Grandma Jan. "Thank you for the offer, Jan, but I'm going to stay with CC."

Grandma Jan reached back into her windbreaker pocket and took out the can of mace. "Here, Anne, I want you to keep this. You can't be too careful. I'll keep an eye on your place." She hugged Anne before walking out the back door.

CC helped Anne board up the kitchen door before Anne put Sassy into the cat carrier.

"Okay," Anne said, gathering up some things, including the cat carrier with Sassy stowed safely inside. She followed CC home.

Chapter Thirty

Anne woke to the sound of a crashing floor lamp and the hiss of a screeching cat. "CC, I forgot to close my bedroom door and Bandit was hot on Sassy's tail," Anne apologized.

After cleaning up the glass, CC washed her hands and cut up strawberries. She combined flour, buttermilk, eggs, a touch of sugar and baking powder. She added the strawberries to the mixture. Testing the griddle with a drop of water, she put the pancakes on the sizzling pan. When the pancakes were done, she topped them with a large spoon of cream cheese and a fresh sprig of basil.

Anne looked at the plate and realized she'd forgotten to turn her filter on. Editing her words had never been her strong suit. Maybe that's why she'd gotten on so well with Sybil. "You don't have any Lingon berries, do you?"

"I don't exactly keep Lingon berries around the house. We'll have to settle for strawberries."

"I'm sure it'll be good."

This was one of those *Anne-syncrasies* that CC wasn't very fond of. She was never quite satisfied.

After breakfast, they headed back to Anne's house to wait for the locksmith. CC stayed until after he'd left. When CC returned home, the phone was ringing. She ran to grab it. "Hello," she said.

"CC?" a tentative voice asked. "This is Marco, Ida's son-in-law," he stuttered.

CC could hear the sadness in his voice. "Yes, Marco, what's wrong?"

"Ida passed last night," he said.

CC threw her purse onto her table and slid onto the dining room chair. Bandit danced around her feet.

Marco continued talking, "She'd been ill for a while. It was a lot worse than she let on. She just went in her sleep."

I'm so sorry. She was such a sweet lady," CC said.

"I wanted to call you and let you know. Ida appreciated your finding the bear for baby Lily. Having you as a friend meant a lot to her." He paused. "The funeral is this Saturday if you can make it."

"I'm so sorry. I'll be there."

Chapter Thirty-One

Anne and CC parked in the circle drive outside Chicago's illustrious Field Museum. They walked up the limestone steps. "You know, Anne, this museum is constructed from steel and Georgian marble and was inspired by Grecian and Roman temples. Originally, it was called the Palace of Fine Arts when it was built for the 1893 Colombian Exposition.

"In 1921, the museum was moved to its present location. It took six years and cost $7 million dollars to build," CC said as they opened the large doors.

Anne didn't hear a word her friend said as she took in the glass display cases and various hallways marked *Egyptian, Jurassic Period.* They walked up to the Help Desk near the ticket booths. "Can we see Wayne Muscarello?" Anne asked.

"Do you have an appointment?" the elderly woman wearing a pink volunteer badge asked.

"No, but he'll recognize the name—Hillstrom. He'll want to see us," Anne said, handing the woman one of their business cards.

"Very well," the woman said, picking up the phone. "Mr. Muscarello, there's a Miss Hillstrom here to see you." She put the phone down and said, "He'll be up shortly."

A few minutes later, a nice looking man in his early fifties with brown hair and a Tom Cruise smile walked up to them. CC was still by the reception desk, Anne had wandered over to look at the British collection currently on loan from the Royal Museum. He walked directly to Anne.

"Anne, how are you?" Muscarello extended his hand. "We were so sorry about your aunt. She will be missed."

Anne shook his hand. "Thank you, Wayne; it's nice to see you again."

"It's nice to see you, too. How can I help you?"

"I've got something I'd like you to take a look at. Actually, two things I want to show you."

"Sure; let's go back to my office to take a look."

CC and Anne followed him down a long corridor. Anne only paused once to stare at a Queen Elizabeth I golden scalloped cameo brooch. "C'mon, Anne." CC grabbed her by the arm and dragged her down the hallway, preventing Anne from lingering at the Italian urns and Egyptian tombs. They made their way down to the lower level where Wayne's office was.

It was a large office, but seemed smaller by the clutter of books and charts that hung on the walls, crowded the shelves, and decorated the desk. Anne felt right at home and began leafing through an old museum catalog. Wayne pulled over two chairs and motioned for them to sit down. He walked behind his desk. "Let's see what you have."

Anne twisted the gold band off her finger and handed it to him.

Looking at it closely, Wayne appeared to recognize the crest inside the band. "This is wonderful. You know this is the Hillstrom crest."

"Yes, I thought it was."

"This is very special. It's the same crest as on the Queen's brooch. They both date to about the ninth century. At that time, the Hillstrom crest was a royal crest. The Hillstroms were in power throughout

Sweden. Generations later, the crest changed when the power changed."

"I guess that's why I didn't recognize it right away. But it looked similar to the Hillstrom crest," Anne said.

"Take a walk with me. You must have seen the rest of the collection." Wayne led them back out of the office into a dark exhibit room which had a glass display case in the center. Standing upright in the case's center was a Viking sword with the royal Hillstrom crest on its hilt. Anne leaned in close to the glass. "I hadn't seen this since I was a little girl. My cousin Suzy and I used to play Viking pirates with that sword until we got caught. I never noticed a difference in the crest," she said.

"I was glad to hear that the brooch wasn't taken in the burglary. Now I'm glad to find out that the ring wasn't taken either," Wayne said.

"Sybil had the brooch in a lock deposit box. I didn't know about it until the attorney gave me the key." Anne paused. "The ring was stolen, and I recovered it."

"That's definitely the ring that goes with the brooch. That was Queen Aldis Hillstrom's wedding band," Wayne said, handing it back to her. "You said you had something else to show me?"

"Oh, yes. Can we go back to your office?" Anne asked. They went back into his office and Anne sank back down onto the chair. Opening her large orange Prada bag, Anne handed him the spoon which she'd wrapped carefully in a soft cotton sock.

Wayne pulled it out and turned it around, looking it over. "Interesting." He turned on his magnifying lamp and put the spoon under it so he could take a closer look. "I've only seen this spoon once before if it's what I think it is." He jumped up and opened a metal chest. He pulled out white cotton gloves. He took a key from the ring on the chain hanging from his pocket. He opened up a glass case pulling out a leather-bound journal.

CC and Anne crowded next to him as he delicately opened the journal. The name on the first page said, "Sam Adams."

"It's a one of a kind journal," Wayne said. "Sam Adams was a member of the Sons of Liberty, the group that planned the Boston tea party."

"Anne and I were just at a Revolutionary War reenactment in Springfield. We're quite familiar with Sam Adams and the Sons of Liberty," CC interrupted. "On our journey downstate, we picked up an authentic Minuteman rifle with the Sons of Liberty symbol."

"I'd love to see that," Wayne said. "I'd be interested in it for my own private collection."

"Let's get back to the spoon. We can talk about guns later," Anne said.

"Yes, back to Sam Adams. He wrote about the Boston tea party." Wayne turned a couple of pages. They saw there a drawing of some men dressed like Indians on a ship—one of them depicted as sitting and drinking tea. Wayne brought over a magnifying glass. "Look closely; you can see the end of the spoon he's stirring the tea with."

Anne looked through the magnifying glass. "That's it! That's my spoon!" she said, about to burst.

"Who's the man who's drinking the tea, holding the spoon?" CC asked.

"That's Paul Revere. I think that the mark on the back is an *R* for Revere."

Anne's heart pounded and she gasped for air. "I have to sit." She sank back into the chair.

Wayne closed the book and got her a cup of water from the cooler. "Are you okay?"

Anne downed the water and crushed the paper cup. "I've seen Paul Revere spoons before, Mr. Muscarello.

None of them were this ornate. They were all very plain. They were made for everyday people," CC said.

Wayne pulled a chair up and sat in front of her. "According to Sam Adams, Paul Revere made that spoon just for the Boston Tea Party. He wanted to make it very ornate as a means of snubbing his nose at King George. According to what I've read, he carried it with him on his famous ride. If this is the spoon, it's priceless."

Anne's heart leapt out of her chest. "It looks exactly like the illustration. This must be the spoon!"

"We'd have to see the provenance. The Paul Revere Tea Party spoon, as I've heard it called, was sold to an anonymous collector several years ago," Wayne said. "That was at Sotheby's in London. The sale was kept confidential. It would be difficult to confirm."

"Is there a way to check on it?" Anne asked.

"I can take pictures of your spoon and email them to my acquaintance at Sotheby's." He took out a digital camera and took photos of the spoon from many different angles.

With the spoon safely back in her purse, Anne and CC followed Wayne back to the front entrance.

"Do you mind if we look around a little?" Anne asked, delighting in the idea of a free museum visit.

"Oh, by all means," Wayne said. "I'll contact you when I hear back from my friend at Sotheby's. It was nice to see you again, Anne. Your aunt spoke highly of you. She will be missed by all of us at the museum."

"Thanks again, Wayne. We appreciate the help." Anne said.

Wayne turned and headed back down the corridor to his office.

"Anne, I really think we should put the spoon in my safety deposit box in case it is the real spoon. It could be worth a fortune," CC said.

"The safest place for it is right here with me. I'm not letting it out of my sight." Anne clutched her large orange Prada bag tightly.

Chapter Thirty-Two

Anne held Suzanne's hand while waiting for the on-duty officer at the Glencoe Police Station. "I'm so glad you've decided to do this," Anne said.

"I don't have a choice. Last night I thought I heard something in the yard. I was sort of knocked out because I'd taken a sleeping pill. I hoped it was just raccoons in the garbage again, but this morning I saw that someone had tried to break in the back door," her cousin said.

"You believe it was Jack, don't you?" Anne asked.

Suzanne nodded her head and her eyes welled with tears. "I know it was him. He's not going to stop until he hurts me. I know it."

"Do you want me to stay with you?"

"No, I have to fight this battle on my own," Suzanne said. "I spent too many years being afraid of him. I'm not going to let him do that to me anymore."

After they'd filed the restraining order against Jack, Anne had driven Suzanne back to Aunt Sybil's house. She'd waited with her while the locksmith changed all the locks. They'd sat drinking lemonade on the white rockers on the front porch. "Anne, I've always loved this house. I think the last time I was truly happy was right here." Suzanne paused and looked out over the front lawn and said, "I'm grateful to Aunt Sybil. She's given my girls and me a chance at a new life."

"I know she would have wanted you to be happy here," Anne said. "We're not going to let Jack take that away from you; I promise. "

"He's taken away so much already. You think the restraining order is enough? I don't even know where he is right now. What if he comes back tonight?"

"The cops are looking for him," Anne said with a confidence she didn't quite feel.

"Why?" Suzanne asked.

"I didn't want to worry you before, but someone broke into my house."

"You think it was Jack?" Suzanne asked. She paused for a moment and then said, "I've seen Jack at his worst. I think if I hadn't left him, he would have killed me. I know he's capable of it."

"Suzanne, do you think Jack killed Sybil?"

"I've thought about it," she replied. "He hated her. We'd asked her to help us before we moved to Minnesota and she wouldn't loan us any money."

"I don't understand." Anne shook her head. "Why did she hire him to work on her house?"

"I called Sybil after Jack and I had a bad fight. I told her I needed her help. She hired Jack so we could make enough money to move back. I told her that once I got back home, I'd have the support I needed to leave Jack." Suzanne paused. "When Jack found out that Sybil was helping me leave him, he was furious."

Chapter Thirty-Three

The white steeple of the Lutheran Trinity Church in New Buffalo, Michigan, pierced the beautiful blue summer sky. The cross on the point of the steeple summoned the faithful. The cornerstone on the outside read, "Man shall not live by bread alone, but on every word that comes from the mouth of God." Anne paused to read it, but CC grabbed her arm and pulled her inside just as the strains of the opening hymn began. "This church was built during the Great Depression to lift the spirits of the community—a way to not only feed their stomachs but their souls," CC whispered as they walked into the nave and searched for an open pew. Most of New Buffalo had come to pay their respects for Ida.

Finding a seat in the back on a creaky pew, Anne admired the stained glass windows. The church relied on the Lake Michigan breeze for air conditioning. It wasn't working. Anne used her bulletin to fan herself. She wasn't very good at wakes and funerals. She had lost both her parents at an early age. Her brother, William, and sister, Katherine, both lived out of state, so Anne had handled the funeral arrangements for both of her parents on her own.

CC dabbed her face with a handkerchief. Luckily, she never used a lot of makeup—or needed to. She felt a little embarrassed that she looked so good in her black dress and pearls. It was the proper funeral attire, but it also accented her curves and made her blue eyes pop. CC wondered if Anne had considered wearing her flowered pants, but had thought better of it at the last minute.

The Reverend started his eulogy, speaking of the many charitable works Ida had performed in her little town and about her beloved family. From behind her, a slight breeze blew the back of CC's hair. She felt a chill down her spine, but the breeze was warm. She turned around and saw Tony Tedesco standing in the entryway making the sign of the cross. She thought that was unusual in a Lutheran church, but then realized he must be Catholic. This was the first time she'd seen him in a tailored suit. Like her, it really highlighted his athletic physique. She immediately shook that thought off as inappropriate for the occasion—but he did look good. His rugged features seemed softer. His eyes glistened a bit. When the Reverend said, "Let us all pray," CC bowed her head and closed her eyes. She could still see the outline of Tony's body. His image burned into the inside of her eyelids like a flash bulb had gone off until it slowly faded away. When the prayer was over, she turned to see him again, but he was gone.

CC wondered why Tony wasn't with his wife. After the service, Anne and CC walked up to the open casket. A group of people had gathered around, chatting quietly. A nicely dressed man walked up to them and introduced himself as Marco. He thanked them for making the trip. Ida's daughter, Rose, was holding baby Lily. "Thank you so much for coming. My mom talked about you and your blog," Rose said. "It really made her happy to read about your adventures. We'd love for you to come back to the house for lunch."

Anne and CC nodded in agreement. They walked outside the church where groups of people were still standing. Tony was leaning against his pickup. "Excuse me, Anne." CC turned and touched Anne's shoulder.

Anne was talking to the Reverend. "Ill be right back." CC walked over to Tony.

"Ida was a great woman. Everybody around here loved her," Tony said.

"I didn't know her that long, but she was a sweetheart," CC said.

"Listen, it might not be the right time to ask, but I don't know when I'm going to see you again. I'd really love for you to come see my boat," Tony said. "The bell is perfect. It's docked ten minutes from here."

In the corner of her eye, CC caught a glimpse of his wedding ring again and thought of walking away. There was something so sad in his eyes. She didn't have the heart to say no. "Let me tell my friend." CC walked back to Anne, talked to her for a few minutes and then returned to Tony.

Tony held open the passenger door for her and they drove off. When they arrived at the harbor, the air was at least ten degrees cooler. She felt refreshed. The calm waters of the harbor gently splashed against the wooden slips. At the end of a long wooden pier was the 41-foot Italian yacht. "It's beautiful," CC said, stepping onto the freshly varnished wooden deck.

"In the shipyard back in Italy where I worked, a customer brought her in. She was in terrible shape, but I could see what she used to be. The beautiful lines. The way she cut the water. I removed all the caulk from all the planks, stripped down all the wood, reinforced the hull and spent 16 months just getting her in good enough condition to put her on the water. The man who brought her in couldn't afford to pay for the repairs so my father-in-law bought it from him." Tony explained as he showed her around the main deck.

"Your father in law?"

"He's the one who gave me the job. He owned the shipbuilding company. He was a master shipwright. He took me in as his apprentice and that's where I met my wife."

"Oh," CC murmured, wrapping her arms around herself.

"Wait, let me show you the bell." He took CC's hand and led her up to the helm. Hanging next to the steering wheel, CC could see the bell.

"It is perfect," she said.

Tony said, "Where are my manners? Can I offer you a glass of wine or something?"

"I better not. I haven't eaten yet. We're invited back to Ida's daughter's house for a luncheon," she paused. "I don't feel comfortable going back there. It's mostly family and close friends."

"Let me make you lunch. It's the least I can do after you found this bell for me. Let me show you the galley." He slid open the teak door and they walked down the narrow stairs into the galley. The whole kitchen was completely remodeled with high-end appliances and work surfaces. *It was intimate,* CC thought.

"It's quite cozy, don't you think?" Tony asked. "Sit, sit." He brought her over to the wooden booth in the corner of the galley. He took his tie and jacket off and rolled up his sleeves. He grabbed an apron and put it on. CC thought he looked quite at home in the kitchen. "Let's get this going." He reached into the wine rack and pulled out a bottle of white. He pulled two wine glasses off the rack hanging over the counter. CC took a sip. "This is really good." She looked at the bottle to see the label but there was none.

"I made that myself. I brought the grapes with me from Italy. They grow very well in this region."

CC took another sip. She was starting to feel more at ease. Tony took some clams out of the small refrigerator and threw them into a boiling pot. He took angel hair pasta, sprinkled in some salt and boiled it for a couple minutes and then threw it all into a cast iron skillet with garlic, olive oil and sea salt.

"That smells great," CC said.

"You can't live in Italy for ten years and not pick up a little something in the kitchen. My wife was a wonderful cook."

"Was?"

Tony was quiet for a minute as he put the clams and angel hair on two plates. He sat down across from CC. He took a sip of his wine. "Apollonia was beautiful. She was 25 when I met her. I was about the same age. I was traveling throughout Europe, doing odd jobs and carpentry. Anything for a meal and a place to sleep. After just drifting with no ambition, I arrived in a little village in Tuscany where I worked on a fishing boat. That's where I met Angelo," he paused, cupping his wine glass in his long, narrow fingers. "He was repairing one of the boats in the village. We talked and I told him that I was a carpenter. He hired me to help. Eventually, I worked as his apprentice in the shipyard. I learned everything about restoring these beautiful yachts. He was an artist. Everything he did was by hand. Even the tools he used he made himself. After a year or so, we became close. He brought me home for dinner. That's when I met Apolonia. As much as Angelo liked and respected me, I could see why he had kept me away from her. She was absolutely beautiful. I fell in love the minute I saw her." Tony stopped, cleared his throat and took another sip of wine.

"I didn't mean to pry."

"It's okay." Tony interrupted. "We had ten wonderful years together. I woke up one morning and she didn't. Doctors said it was a brain aneurysm. All the joy went out of my life. I couldn't stay in Italy. Everything reminded me of her. Angelo could see my heart would never heal as long as I stayed there. He gave me this boat. That's when I brought her back to America and wound up working at the Chicago Yacht Club. And eventually opened my shop here." As he held his wine glass, he stared at his wedding band. He could see CC was staring at it also. "I can't bring myself to take it off. If I take it off, it's too real. It means she's really gone."

CC tried to hold back the tears. It was such a sad but beautiful story. She'd never felt love like that. She didn't realize there was a love like that in the world. It made her sad for him and sad for herself.

Chapter Thirty-Four

Anne strolled the aisles of the dusty antique store. It was the only one she could find open after putting in a brief appearance at the luncheon. She was a little upset with CC for abandoning her, but browsing through the crystal made it a little easier. She picked up a silver creamer, marveling at its elaborate engraving. "Silver," she said to herself. It was making her crazy thinking about the spoon in her purse. She wondered how much longer CC would be. She wondered if people browsing down the aisle beside her realized that she might be carrying a priceless piece of American history.

Putting the creamer down, she thought she might have the matching sugar bowl somewhere in her collection at home. She'd have to find it and then come back to get this mate. She pulled the long list out of her vintage Chanel black bag, making sure to close the bag securely. "Thank God, I had the spoon with me when the house was broken into," Anne said, stopping in her tracks. With all the valuables she had in her house, whoever broke in hadn't taken anything. Anne had taken a complete inventory and triple checked it. They obviously were looking for something and didn't find it. Of course, they didn't find it because Anne had it! Someone was looking for the spoon! She couldn't wait to tell CC her revelation. "Where is she?" she asked herself impatiently, looking at her watch.

Since the *Chicago Tribune* article had been released, their list had grown substantially. Requests had come in from fans across the country. Anne believed it was her mission to find all the items on the list. Scanning CC's scrawling handwriting, she read through the items and then looked around the store. It was the second time she'd taken a complete tour of the store.

"Mystery Date," she pondered. "I think I saw that somewhere in here." Anne strolled along and found the area where old toys were stacked. In the back corner, she could make out the distinctive white box of the 1960s board game. Removing the boxes covering it, she grabbed the box. *One item off the list*, she thought, looking at her watch again. *Where is CC?*

She reached back into her purse and pulled out Detective Tower's business card. A little reluctant to bother him on a Sunday, but with the thought of someone coming after her spoon, she felt a sense of urgency. Nigel picked up after the third ring. "Detective Towers," the British-accented voice came through the phone. Whenever Anne heard Nigel's voice, she thought about *Doctor Who*. She'd always wanted a full-size Tardis.

"Nigel, I'm sorry to bother you on a Sunday. This is Anne Hillstrom," she said, tentatively.

"Oh, not a problem. I wasn't doing much of anything."

"I don't know exactly how important this is, but it's about my spoon."

The detective paused. "Spoon? Huh?"

"It's a long story but I think the burglars may have been looking for my spoon. It could be very valuable." As a woman brushed past her, Anne cupped her hand around the phone and whispered into it. She walked outside. "I believe a spoon that I bought from Tim Whitmore's estate sale could be a very valuable Paul Revere silver spoon worth a small fortune."

"I see," Detective Towers said. "How would someone know about the spoon?"

"That's the thing," Anne said. "I overheard someone at another estate sale asking about a silver spoon. I think they were talking about my spoon."

"Anne, I think it might be better if we meet in person, and you can show me the spoon," the detective said.

"Of course, Nigel. I'm in Michigan right now. Should I come into the station on Monday?"

"That's not necessary. I can pop on by your house."

"Okay; that would be lovely," Anne said. She hung up the phone and went back into the antique store.

On the boat, CC offered to help wash dishes. "No, they're fine," Tony said as he placed them in the sink.

"I appreciate lunch. It was fantastic but Anne's waiting for me," CC said, taking her cell phone from her purse and seeing several missed calls and text messages asking if she was still alive. The last one was in all caps—Anne's version of shouting.

"We have to finish this bottle first," Tony said. "It would be a shame to recork it." He grabbed CC's hand and helped her up the short stairway to the deck. It was a lipstick sunset. The red setting sun smeared itself across the darkened blue summer sky. The water glistened. There was a delicious cool breeze. Tony filled both glasses, handing one to CC. The only sound was the gentle kiss of the waves against the boat. CC felt like they were the only two people on the lake. The man on the train stirred something inside her that she'd never felt before.

Anne perched on the curb outside the antique store. She had long stopped trying to reach CC and had actually thought about taking off for home without her friend. Of course, that wouldn't be the right thing to do. She swatted another mosquito. Everything was closed.

It was nearly 8 p.m., on a Sunday, and all the sidewalks had been rolled up.

Anne was angry and worried. Just when she was about to give up, she saw a truck turn the corner and enter the parking lot. CC flew out of the passenger door. "Anne, I'm so sorry!" she cried before turning around to wave good-bye to Tony.

"I was worried sick about you, CC. You couldn't call me back? Text me? Nothing?" Anne stood, picking her bags up. "Where have you been all this time?"

They both got into CC's car. "Time got away from me. Tony wanted to show me the bell and the boat. It's a beautiful boat and the bell is perfect." CC started the car.

"And?" Anne asked.

"And?" CC said. "He wanted to thank me, so we had lunch. We had some wine, and it was nice."

"Nice?" Anne asked.

"It was nice. He's a nice guy." CC stared straight ahead as she drove back to the highway.

"Oh." Anne paused. "Oh, yes. I talked to Detective Towers."

"What for?"

"About the spoon. I'd never told him about the spoon before. It makes sense to me now. Why all of a sudden would someone break into my house and not take anything? Just toss everything around? They were looking for something, CC. What would I have that someone would break into my house to look for? The spoon! It has to be the spoon."

CC thought about it. It seemed to make sense. She agreed that everything seemed to be happening since Anne brought the spoon home. "Jared didn't know anything about it. But Banning seemed very interested in finding it," she said to Anne.

"You think?" Anne asked. "Do you think Banning found out I bought it and broke into my house?"

"That doesn't make sense," CC said. "If Banning knew the value of the spoon, he never would have left it at the estate sale. And he obviously knows the value of antiques. He handled all of Whitmore's collections—or at least that's what Jared said. Who else knows about the spoon?"

Anne was afraid to tell CC what she was really thinking. She remembered the look in Jack's eyes at the attorney's office. She knew Jack was capable of hurting someone—or even worse.

Chapter Thirty-Five

Detective Towers was wearing his pink paisley tie. He felt sometimes that because of his height and his gaunt features that people were intimidated or even a bit frightened by him. He'd been teased about it mercilessly as a child growing up in Liverpool, always a foot taller than the other boys. He was never very good at sports. He spent most of his time reading or watching old movies. He loved Americana but now, after ten years as a Chicago police officer, he'd found the reality was not equal to the Hollywood version. He had seen a lot of human tragedy and not very much human kindness. As he drove to Anne Hillstrom's house, he hoped he would be able to help her.

When he pulled into the driveway, he saw Anne sitting on the swing on the porch. She was wearing those flowered pants. He'd thought once or twice about her and those pants since their last meeting. He ducked his head down to get out of the Crown Vic. His knees almost touched his chin. As he slipped through the driver's door, he called out, "Miss Hillstrom!"

"Anne, please," she said, getting up to greet the detective as he walked up the stairs. "I like your tie." They walked inside into the kitchen. "Nigel, please sit down."

Nigel sat across from Anne. She poured them a cup of tea and then unwrapped the spoon with a flourish and handed it to the detective. "Lovely craftsmanship," he said. "It looks early American."

"I believe it's a Paul Revere," Anne said.

"And you believe that this is what the burglar was after?"

Anne nodded and said, "It could be priceless."

"Do you have the provenance?"

"No, I bought it at an estate sale. It didn't have a price sticker or any information. The person who I bought it from charged me $5."

"The first thing you need to do is find out what it is," the detective said.

"How do you propose we do that?" Anne asked.

"You can start by verifying the silver content," Nigel said. "I can take it to the lab. It might take a while to get it back."

She grabbed the spoon from his bony fingers. "No, you don't. It's not leaving my sight." She paused. "Sorry, Nigel, I didn't mean to be so rude. I'm a chemist. I can test it in my lab."

"I have a better idea." He got up and took a magnet off her refrigerator. "Can I see the spoon?"

She handed it to him.

He placed the magnet on the spoon, and it stuck. "There appears to be a high level of nickel in this spoon. It's not sterling silver. Paul Revere would have used pure silver."

Anne didn't want to hear it. "If it's not real, why would someone want to steal it?"

"We don't know for sure if that's what they were after. Are you sure nothing was taken?" the detective looked around the cluttered room.

"I am absolutely positive. I've checked every room, every box, every closet. Things were out of sorts and misplaced, but nothing is missing."

Detective Towers was not helping. He could see what the spoon meant to her and, once again, was the bearer of bad news. He had become a police officer to help people.

"If they weren't after the spoon, what were they after?" Anne asked.

"Is it possible there's an old boyfriend or acquaintance? Someone who would have a grudge?"

It had been many years since Anne had dated. She had more or less given up on relationships. She flipped through her mental Rolodex. She'd never been in a relationship long enough to harbor resentment. She couldn't imagine anyone would be angry enough to break in. "No, no one whom I can think of," she said, and thought, *other than Jack.*

Her words surprised the detective. She was a very attractive woman and seemed very sweet. "I think this might just be a case of a random breaking and entering. Maybe when you came home, you startled them. Maybe a car drove by. It wasn't a professional. In most cases, if someone kicks in a door like that, there's not a lot of planning involved. They probably saw that no one was home. Your lights were off and your house is set away from the street. I don't think there's much more of a motive other than opportunity. I'd suggest you get an alarm system, or maybe put your lights on a timer. Anything that will prevent this from happening again."

Anne half listened to the detective. Her scientific mind always looked for answers. She needed to know why. She didn't like to leave questions hanging in the air. Questions were meant to be answered; mysteries were meant to be solved. "Thank you, Nigel," Anne said as she stood and walked him toward the new kitchen door. "I really appreciate your coming over and looking at the spoon. Wait! I forgot; there's something I want to show you in the garage!"

They walked down the back steps to the garage and Anne lifted the heavy overhead door. She made her way to the back of the garage. All Nigel could see was the top of her head occasionally bobbing up. She made it back through the maze, carrying a framed movie poster of James Cagney in the 1931 classic *The Public Enemy*. "It's just a reproduction, but a very good one. Since you enjoy American black and white movies, and the whole Chicago tie-in backdrop, I thought you might like it," she said, handing him the poster.

"Aces," Nigel said. "It's awesome!"

"I wanted to thank you for all your help and knew you'd appreciate the poster."

"I really do." He paused. "The Music Box Theater is having their annual Film Noir festival. It's smashing." Nigel worked very hard to temper his British accent and phrases, but somehow Anne brought the Brit out of him. "Maybe we could go together?"

She looked down at the ground. "That would be lovely."

After she watched him drive away, Anne went back through the back door, closed and locked it. She sat down at the kitchen table. She tried the magnet again. A twenty-nine cent refrigerator magnet was not adequate proof to toss her dreams aside. What she needed was an acid test, even though it meant it might mar the spoon.

She gathered up the spoon and headed to the lab. She donned her rubber gloves and put on safety goggles before taking the spoon out of her purse. Filing a small portion on the back of the handle, she took an eye dropper and put a small drop of nitric acid on the filed part. It turned a milky grayish color, indicating that the spoon was solid silver, but not sterling. If it was a Paul Revere spoon, it should have turned milky white, validating a ninety percent pure silver content. Her heart sunk. As she examined the small filing, she noticed that the spoon was tarnished only on its bowl. She wondered why the rest of the spoon did not show the same evidence of tarnishing. Now that she knew it wasn't an authentic Paul Revere spoon, she filed off a little piece of the bowl to do another chemical analysis. The results came back with the usual sulfide, chloride and nitrate mixture. She also expected to see traces of arsenic, which is common to silver, but the arsenic levels on her spoon's bowl were off the chart! She remembered reading about Chinese emperors who only dined with silver chopsticks to test for poison in their food. If arsenic was present in the food, the silver would tarnish. This spoon had been exposed to a high level of arsenic and whoever ate from it had experienced deadly results. Anne rushed to CC's house to share her findings.

Chapter Thirty-Six

CC was taking pictures of items they'd found and emailing them to people on the list, when Anne burst into her house. Catching her breath, she plopped down next to a surprised CC who looked up from her laptop. Anne caught her breath. "CC, I've tested the spoon! It's definitely not a Paul Revere spoon," Anne said. "It's not even sterling silver."

"Anne, I was afraid of that. I'm very sorry." CC said, closing her laptop.

"I noticed," she said as she pulled the spoon out of her purse, "that only the bowl is tarnished. There's little discoloration on the rest of the spoon. So I took a sample at the lab. It came back with large traces—deadly traces—of arsenic."

"Arsenic is common in silver."

"Not at these levels. These levels are enough to stop your heart," Anne said, pausing. "How did Tim Whitmore die?"

CC opened her laptop, clicked on Google and searched for Tim Whitmore's obituary. "It says he was only 53 when he died of an apparent heart attack." Both girls sat silent as the words *heart attack* sunk in. "Are you saying Tim was murdered?" CC asked.

"I'm not saying that, but how else do you explain the arsenic on the spoon? How else do you explain someone breaking into my house and taking nothing? How else would you explain Whitmore's antique dealer, Banning, being frantic about finding the spoon?"

"Anne, you can't prove any of that."

Anne sat back in the chair. "This is all wrong." The spoon was a fake. Tim Whitmore was dead. She needed to figure out how it all was connected. This wasn't a fast-moving train out of the Orient or hounds of the Baskervilles, but it was her chance to bring the puzzle pieces together. She'd spent her life breaking down elements to their purest form, understanding how parts come together to make a whole. Now she'd do the same for this problem. Like any formula, putting the right ingredients together creates the solution. "CC, we need to work backwards from what we know to what we don't know."

"What are you talking about?"

"We need to find out why someone would murder Tim Whitmore."

"No, what we need to do is go to the cops."

"You said it yourself. There's no proof. What are we going to tell them?"

"You can show them the spoon."

Anne pulled out her cell phone and dialed Detective Towers. "Nigel," she said into the phone.

"Nigel?" CC questioned, giving Anne a sharp glance.

Anne corrected herself. "Detective Towers, it's Anne Hillstrom."

"Hello, Anne."

"Detective, I wanted to come talk to you more about the spoon."

"Anne, I'm sorry that the spoon is a fake. There's not much more I can do for you."

"That's not it. I tested the spoon," she said. "I found large quantities of arsenic."

"Did you find old lace also?" he said with dry British humor.

"Nigel, I'm not kidding," Anne said.

"Anne, after you showed me the spoon, I checked on Tim Whitmore's file. He died of natural causes. He had a history of heart problems. There's no evidence of foul play."

"Then how do you explain the arsenic?"

"I don't, Anne, but that's not my department. That would be homicide. The case has already been closed. And, I'll tell you, it would take a lot to open it again. They just don't have the manpower." He paused. "Besides that, Tim Whitmore was cremated a week ago. Without a body, there's no crime."

"Thanks, detective; sorry to have bothered you." Anne hung up the phone. She turned and looked at CC. "Tim was cremated." She paused. "That doesn't matter anyway, because arsenic would have dissolved by now."

CC thought for a moment. "None of that matters with what we've read about Tim Whitmore; he was a heavy smoker and drinker. Detective Towers said he had a history of heart problems. He might have been one cigarette or one cheeseburger away from a heart attack anyway." She paused and asked, "What do you think we should do?"

"CC, I never told you where I found the spoon. I was rummaging—I mean looking—around Tim's bedroom."

"It was off limits. Why'd you go in there?"

"Just curiosity. I was admiring some of his collections and I happened to notice an ashtray next to the bed on his nightstand. It was a beautiful ashtray made from Milano hand-blown glass," Anne recalled. "Oh, and I saw something sticking out from under the bed. It was a linen courier pouch like the re-enactors had in Springfield, remember?"

"Yes?"

"That's where I found the spoon. There was a leather pouch inside with tea leaves in it. We have to go back. I have to test those leaves for arsenic. That would be the proof we need to take to the police."

Chapter Thirty-Seven

As they pulled up in front of the Whitmore estate, they saw a woman clad in a business suit attaching a *For Sale* sign onto the wrought iron gate. They drove past, trying not to seem suspicious and watched her from the end of the road. The gates opened, and the woman in the black Lexus drove in.

"Here's our chance," Anne said.

They got out of the car and walked in before the double gates closed. Making their way along the wooded driveway, staying off the main path and ducking behind bushes and trees. "This is ridiculous," CC said.

"Ssh," Anne said, holding her finger over her lips.

"Anne, why did you have to wear those pants? You can be seen from a mile away."

"They're my lucky pants," Anne retorted.

They watched from the safety of the knock-out rosebushes as the real estate lady opened curtains and windows. They waited in the bushes for what seemed like hours. "So, what are we going to do now?"

"I brought some packing tape. We'll put a little tape over the door lock so the hammer doesn't close all the way when she leaves," Anne said.

"Okay," CC replied.

"Then I brought flashlights and these plastic booties to put over our shoes so we don't leave footprints. And here's your gloves." Anne reached into her backpack.

"Is this all necessary? Our fingerprints are probably already all over the house from the sale."

"To catch a criminal, we have to think like a criminal."

"Okay."

"Now we have to wait until she leaves." Anne reached into her bag. "I brought two-way radios so we can search the whole house and talk to each other."

"But. . .."

"CC, I told you we have to think like criminals. . ."

"But, she's having an open house. There are cars coming. We can just walk in," CC said, pointing to the driveway where a few high-end luxury cars were pulling in.

Anne turned around to see agents with prospective buyers entering the mansion. She was actually disappointed. She didn't like when plans changed and had no tolerance for it. The attractive agent met CC and Anne at the door. "Hi, we saw the *For Sale* sign and we wanted to take a look around," Anne said.

"Are you an agent? Are you looking for yourself? Do you have an agent?" She smiled politely.

"We don't have an agent, but we're very interested in the property."

"Come on in; here's my card. I'm Rita." She handed them a business card as they walked past her into the large entryway. She gave Anne a sideways glance. "I really like your pants. Are those Lily Pulitzer?"

"Oh, no; they're one of a kind," Anne said, giving CC a look of *I told you so.*

"Lovely," Rita replied, looking over her shoulder as she walked past them back to the kitchen.

They headed to the bedroom upstairs but were waylaid by a hand-carved teak Chinese trunk. "I don't remember seeing this at the estate sale." Anne ran her hand along the ornate carved lines. The house had been cleared out from the sale, but as they walked they found other new antiques. "I don't remember seeing this either." Anne pointed at an alabaster urn filled with silk willow reeds. It was on the landing. "Tim Whitmore had a really good eye for antiques. These are nice pieces."

"Oh, those are all for sale also. Let me know if there's something you're interested in; I can contact Mr. Ripley for you. He's the estate sales manager," Rita called up to them from the bottom of the stairs.

"Yes, we were at the sale. We didn't see these pieces then," Anne said.

"A lot of Mr. Whitmore's collection was stored in his warehouse, and Mr. Ripley just brought them over for staging," Rita replied.

"These are very nice pieces. Mr. Whitmore was quite a collector," CC said.

"Actually, his antique dealer, Mr. Banning, bought all the pieces. Mr. Whitmore hired him right after he won the Powerball. I see a lot of houses on the North Shore. I actually sold this house to Tim. Let's just say he was more at home in a trailer park than on the North Shore, but he wanted to fit in so he hired Banning to decorate the house. If you're interested in these pieces, there's a warehouse filled with antiques but I'd have to put you in touch with Banning."

"Thank you. We're just going to take a quick look upstairs."

"Certainly. I'm here if you need me."

"I hope it's still here," Anne whispered as they reached the top landing. Entering the master bedroom, she glanced around. The room had been emptied out but the four-poster bed remained. Anne rushed over and knelt down looking underneath it. She retrieved the carrier pouch. "It's here!" she held the pouch up triumphantly.

"Put that away before someone sees us," CC hissed.

Anne stuffed the pouch into her large orange Prada bag. "Let's get out of here," CC said, grabbing Anne's hand and leading her back down the stairs.

"Wait. I want to look around a little bit to see if we missed anything else," Anne protested, stopping and bumping into a couple wandering around the house.

"Are you crazy?" CC asked. "We have to get out of here." She opened the front door and pulled Anne down the stairs behind her. They were in such a hurry that they weren't watching where they were walking. As they opened the door, they bumped straight into Banning.

Anne dropped her large orange Prada bag. Banning knelt down and picked it up. Holding the purse tightly in both hands, he stared at Anne with what appeared to be a deep sense of recognition that made Anne feel uncomfortable. She murmured, "Thank you," in a timid voice and reached for her purse.

Banning hesitated and handed it back to her without a word. He then walked into the house.

Anne and CC rushed to the car and headed straight to the lab.

Anne completed her chemical analysis of the tea leaves and, as she suspected, they were laced with arsenic—a heavy dose of arsenic. "What do we do now?" Anne asked CC.

"We have to bring everything to the police. Tim Whitmore was murdered," CC said, staring over Anne's shoulder at the results of the chemical analysis on the computer screen.

"I still don't think there's enough to convince them."

"It's not our job to convince them," CC said.

But Anne wasn't listening. Anne was realizing the woman she wanted to be. The little girl who imagined herself as Nancy Drew had suddenly become a woman imagining herself as Miss Marple. All her childhood books and adolescent dreams were becoming reality. It was frightening, but exciting. For the first time in many years, Anne felt a purpose. She felt all her years unraveling small mysteries in a lab had not been wasted. She could make a difference, she would make a difference!

"CC, the real estate agent said that Whitmore had a warehouse full of antiques," Anne said. "Tim Whitmore's murder must be connected to his collection. All roads lead to Banning. We just have to go to that warehouse!"

Chapter Thirty-Eight

It wasn't hard for CC to locate Tim Whitmore's storage facility. It was a two-story building in a rundown Chicago neighborhood. Many of the nearby apartment buildings were vacant and boarded up. The only inhabitants on the streets were feral cats and dogs and, of course, the giant Chicago sewer rats. "Why would he pick this neighborhood to store valuable antiques?" Anne asked, looking at the two-story brick fortress that had once been home to a cosmetics manufacturer. It was located behind the overhead EL tracks, a perfect lair to hide secrets. The frequent cackle of the Chicago EL train helped cover their noise.

Anne had learned her lesson from their last attempted break in and didn't wear her flowered pants today. She was wearing a Michael Kors velour tracksuit—all in black—and she'd wrapped a black Muslim hijab scarf around her neck to hide her pasty white Swedish skin.

CC shot her a glance and said, "It's a good place to hide something that you don't want to be found. Who's going to want to come down here?"

The two-story building was surrounded by a 10-foot-high wrought iron fence with curled barbed wire at the top. The girls waited in the shadows until after midnight. It just seemed like the right time to break into the warehouse. It was late enough where there wouldn't be any foot traffic, but not too late so as to look suspicious. The sliding chain link gate was held closed by a thick chain and lock.

The lone streetlight that hung near the front of the gate was too much of a risk. Anne and CC followed the fence around to the back of the warehouse. CC pulled out her bolt cutter, but it barely made a dent in the wrought iron. She nodded at Anne who opened her aluminum briefcase, putting on her protective gloves and goggles. She then pulled out a small bottle of liquid nitrogen. "Stand back," she said to CC. She carefully poured the liquid nitrogen onto one of the iron bars. In seconds, the bars shrunk and started to shred. With one snap of the bolt cutters, they were in.

The heavy steel door of the old factory presented a bigger challenge. It had a skeleton key hole. CC came well prepared. From the city blueprints CC had pulled, she knew the best way to break in. She pulled a large ring of keys from her bag, the ones she'd purchased in Sauganash. She found the right one and the door clicked open.

They turned on their flashlights. "What's that smell?" Anne asked, walking into the building. It had a chemical undertone but she couldn't make it out.

CC sniffed. "It could be acetone. This building was used to manufacture nail polish and other cosmetics. Acetone is used in polish remover. Even though it's been closed, the smell lingers."

Scanning the room with their flashlights, the large cement floor was empty except for a couple of overturned wooden pallets and broken shipping crates. "There's nothing here," Anne whispered.

Tiptoeing, they worked their way over to the steel staircase. Their footsteps echoed as they climbed to the second floor. This floor was packed to the ceiling with crates stenciled with the words *Fragile* and *Handle with Care*. Sliding into the room, CC bumped into a stack of boxes. They teetered, threatening to tumble. Anne hung onto them, wanting to protect the valuables inside.

A tall bronze statue of a timber wolf partially draped with a tarp stood in the center of the room. CC pulled off the tarp. "This is an Edward Kerney. The sculptor who did the lions at the Art Institute," she marveled.

They shined both their flashlights on it to get a better look. CC had spent many hours at the Art Institute and many of those admiring the bronze lions that graced the museum's entrance. She ran her finger delicately along the lines of the timber wolves' back and tail. Unlike the lions, these curves were not as smooth and refined. She shined the light on the wolves' eyes; they didn't have the same depth, the same soul that the art institute lions had. "Anne, this is a fake," CC said. She walked over to a half-opened crate and pulled out an Egyptian alabaster vase. "This isn't Egyptian. It's a replica. It's not even alabaster." She continued opening boxes, lifting tarps with all the same results. CC sat down cross-legged on an empty pallet. "It's the island of misfit toys. Everything is a poor imitation of what it should be."

Anne joined her on the pallet. "Why would Tim Whitmore have a warehouse full of fakes? He could afford the real thing. His house was full of the real thing." Anne touched her head, something felt wet. "Something dripped on my head." She sniffed her finger. "It doesn't smell like nail polish remover."

Together, they shined their flashlights up at the ceiling. The entire rafters of the second floor were spider webbed with cloth soaked in accelerant. Anne couldn't make out the pungent odor. "What is that?" Anne asked.

"I don't know but we better get out of here!"

They heard the slam of a door echoing throughout the hollow building.

By the time they made their way to the staircase, the bottom floor was engulfed in flames. The dark smoke billowed up the stairway. CC grabbed Anne's arm and turned around, heading back up the stairs. Both held their hands over their mouths, trying to keep from breathing in the thickening smoke. "Anne, follow me!" CC ran to one of the barred windows. "We can't go down the stairs. We're going to have to climb out this way!"

Anne reached into her briefcase. "I'm out of liquid nitrogen." She pulled the empty can out of the case.

CC pulled the bolt cutters out of her backpack. She ran her hand up and down the one-inch bars that guarded the window. "I'll never be able to cut through these in time," she said, reaching down to the bottom of one of the bars. "This building was built in 1940 during World War II. Steel was in such high demand for the war effort that the domestic steel was a lower grade," CC said.

"Just hurry! Just cut it already," Anne urged, looking back over her shoulder as the flames ripped through the wood floor. Out of the corner of her eye, she noticed the gleam of what appeared to be a Phoenix glass vase sticking up out of a crate. Bending down to pick it up, she wrapped it in the scarf from her neck and stuffed it in CC's backpack.

"What are you doing?" CC asked.

"Evidence, CC, evidence," Anne said.

"The welding points will be the weakest." CC felt around the bars. "They should be somewhere at the bottom. Aha, here they are!" The two girls each grabbed a handle of the bolt cutter and pushed as hard as they could. The smoke was getting worse. The oak floor was starting to burn and fall apart in places. Flames shot up through the planks. With a final push, the welding point cracked. They snapped two more bars just enough to squeeze through and exit onto the narrow ledge that ran along the length of the building. Anne stuck halfway out the window. "Treadmill!" she screamed. "Treadmill!"

CC tugged until Anne was free and out the window by her side. "Look, the fire escape." CC pointed to the drop-down staircase as they heard the wail of the fire engines in the distance. Clinging tightly to the ledge, they pigeon-walked over to the sliding fire escape ladder. "I can't hold on much longer," Anne said, huffing heavily.

Behind them a glass window exploded outwards from the pressure. Anne moved faster toward the ladder. Lifting her leg over the bar, CC stood on the landing and pulled the ladder down so it hovered just above ground level. She helped Anne climb onto the landing. They climbed down the ladder and disappeared into the night. If they hadn't been in such a hurry, they would have seen a black Mercedes parked down the street.

Chapter Thirty-Nine

CC gazed out her office window that looked over Lake Michigan. Watching the boats skip along the waves, she thought about Tony and their afternoon. She reached for her iPhone and scrolled through her contact list. It hovered over his name. Was she ready for the next step? Was he ready? "This is silly," she said out loud. She typed, "Next time you're in Chicago, I want to return the favor and cook for you." She hit send before she could give it a second thought.

She went back to her cover story on the steel industry's support of the Boy Scouts. Every so often her glance would turn back to her iPhone. When it vibrated, she jumped, only to see Anne's face appear. She read the text, "What happened last night?"

"Someone was trying to burn down the warehouse," CC texted back.

"Why would they want to burn down the warehouse?" Anne's response was almost instant.

"Why was the warehouse full of fake antiques?" CC typed back.

"What do we do now?"

"We can't go to the police. We're criminals now," CC typed back.

"What do we do?" Anne typed again.

"For now, we play it cool. We don't say or do anything until we know who's behind it," CC typed back. "Talk to u soon."

It was almost 5 p.m., and she'd miss her train if she didn't leave. Gathering her purse, she picked up the phone and it vibrated in her hand, startling her. The text message came up, "I'm in Chicago now."

She texted Tony her address. "Dinner at 7 p.m."

"See you," his response came back.

Bandit was glad to see her. They went out into the garden—Bandit to harvest bees while she gathered herbs and flowers. In the kitchen, CC gathered the ingredients for her famous crab and shrimp crepes. She made a very thin crepe batter, put it in the refrigerator to chill and then worked on the roux that formed the base for the shrimp and crab. She added onions and garlic to the flour and butter mixture. Then she heated the crepe pan. She melted the Swiss cheese with some cream. After combining all the ingredients, she put them in the oven to cook. Looking at herself in the mirror, she shuddered. "I look a mess," she said to herself, eying her sweaty brow and white flour-streaked hair. She ran up the stairs and showered quickly. Rifling through her closet, she found a green flowered sundress and put it on. She fixed her makeup, put on heels and went back downstairs to make a green salad.

The doorbell rang. Bandit danced around her feet, barking as she opened the door. Tony was wearing a crisp white button-down shirt that accented his deeply tanned chest. His ocean blue eyes sparkled. He was holding a bouquet of wildflowers and a bottle of his homemade wine. "Am I late?" he said.

CC smiled and said, "You're perfect. You're right on time. C'mon on in."

Bandit gave Tony a good sniff over and concluded he was okay to enter the house. Tony squatted down and gave Bandit's soft fur a massage. Bandit thanked him with a kiss and a head butt. This guy was okay.

Tony walked into the kitchen where CC was filling a Waterford vase with water and sugar. She arranged the wildflowers in the vase. "These are beautiful," she said not turning around from the kitchen sink.

"Can I help?"

"You can open the wine." She looked over her shoulder and nodded toward a kitchen drawer. "The corkscrew is in there."

Tony opened the wine and grabbed two glasses from the cabinet above the sink, filling them. CC brought the vase to the dining room table. "I hope you're hungry," she said.

"I'm starving," he said. "It smells really good."

"Please sit."

He sat at the dining room table and watched CC go to the sideboard and bring out her Limoges china and Reed and Barton flatware. She bent down to the lower cabinet to find her napkin rings. She pulled out two sterling silver napkin rings and two linen napkins. Reaching around Tony's shoulder, she placed one next to his plate, her soft brown hair fell against his cheek. She took longer than was necessary to place the napkin and the holder just right. Tony sat silently, enjoying the show and took a sip. He drank both CC and the wine in. CC fluttered off to the kitchen. She carried the crepes back to the table, setting one plate in front of Tony. She sat down folding her napkin on her lap.

Tony leaned over the plate and inhaled deeply. "This smells great, CC."

"It's a recipe I picked up when I studied in France."

"Did you go to culinary school?"

"I was in college and did a semester abroad. I took cooking classes at a French college."

"It smells delicious. Do you mind if I say grace?" Tony asked.

It had been a while since CC had prayed. She was used to eating meals by herself. It was nice to share the ritual of dining. He took CC's hand in his, said a short prayer in Italian and concluded with *Amen.*

"Amen," CC repeated.

Tony looked at her. "Sorry, it's been a while since I've said grace in English. The translation in Italian means 'Thank you for the harvest and for the company.'"

After enjoying the meal and light conversation, Tony asked, "Tell me about your blog. How'd you get started?"

"It started as a whim. My friend, Anne, and I enjoy going to estate sales and we wanted to share our experiences with other enthusiasts. That's how I met Ida. After the story about Ida and the bear appeared in the paper, we started receiving a lot of requests."

"Requests?"

"Like your ship bell. People looking for items, childhood memorabilia, special gifts for loved ones. Items that are hard to find. The list is getting overwhelming."

"Maybe I can help."

"Ooh, wait." She jumped up, got her laptop and brought it to the table. Scrolling down the list, she read. "I remember seeing this Kristin from Iowa. Her husband's retired. He was an insurance broker. His hobby is woodworking. He's built a whole shop in her garage. He's very much into handcrafting furniture using antique tools. She hasn't been able to find any woodworking tools."

"I've got a whole ship full of them. I've got irons that I've made, miter boxes, Italian handsaws, chisels, more than I can use."

"That's great. Maybe you can send me some pictures, and we can see if that will help her out. Of course, I'll give you whatever she pays us."

"Pay?"

"Yes, we've been charging for the item plus a small finder's fee. It was Anne's idea."

They finished the bottle of wine. CC led Tony out to the gazebo in the backyard. The sweet smell of the peonies wafted in on the warm summer breeze. The full moon lit the backyard. The crickets serenaded their lonesome tune. They sat on the cedar glider bench and rocked instinctively to the crickets' song.

Chapter Forty

Anne sat in her favorite chair staring at the Phoenix glass vase she'd grabbed from the warehouse. *Rising from the ashes*, she thought. After a five-minute examination, she knew right away it was a fake. A very good fake, but a fake nonetheless. What really bothered her was that she remembered seeing the vase before but couldn't remember where. When it came to antiques, she had a pretty good memory of everything she'd bought, wanted to buy or was going to buy. Her French ormolu mantle clock struck 9 p.m. She marveled at the gold leaf clock for a moment and then realized she hadn't eaten dinner. She was starving. She was on her fifth fad diet. With all the recent stress in her life, she decided to cheat just this once. For some reason, she had a craving for pancakes. Unlike her best friend, Anne didn't like to cook. She went to the freezer, pulled out some frozen pancakes and put them in the toaster oven. While they were heating up, she grabbed some butter and syrup. "Buttersworth!" she cried out loud, dropping the syrup bottle to the floor. "Betsy Buttersworth was carrying it at the Whitmore estate sale!"

For the first time in a long time, CC couldn't think of anything to say. It wasn't an uncomfortable silence. It was the opposite. It was a very comfortable silence. She was enjoying just being with Tony. Nothing could ruin this moment. "CC! CC!" she heard a voice screaming from the kitchen. Anne came flying out the back door, waving her arms madly, the vase precariously balanced in her arm.

"Is that a friend of yours?" Tony asked, looking at CC.

"Sometimes," she whispered back.

They both stood up. Anne ran up to them, huffing and puffing, giving Tony a onceover. "You're Tony," she said.

"Yes, I am."

"I'm Anne, CC's best friend."

CC rolled her eyes.

Tony shook Anne's hand. "Is everything okay?" he asked

"Yes." Anne inhaled deeply. "I must talk to CC immediately. It's of the utmost importance."

Tony turned to CC, pulling his car keys out of his pocket. "I had a really nice time. Dinner was great."

"You don't have to go. I can get rid of her."

Anne crossed her arms and hpmhed.

"I have to drive to New Buffalo tonight. I have to open the shop in the morning," he said.

"I'll walk you out."

"Oh, no; this seems really important. I can find my way out."

They stood awkwardly for a moment, looking at each other before Tony walked out the cedar back gate.

"Okay, Anne, thanks for ruining my night." CC turned and gave Anne a glare.

"CC, this is really important." Anne sank down onto the edge of the glider. "I grabbed a Phoenix vase when we left the warehouse. It's fake like the rest of the stuff in the warehouse."

"Ok. And?"

"I was making pancakes."

"Pancakes? I thought you were back on the low carb diet."

"Not now, CC, this is important. Anyway, I was making pancakes, and I went to get some syrup. I remembered Buttersworth. Betsy Buttersworth was carrying a vase exactly like this one at the Whitmore sale. We have to find out if her vase is real."

"How are we going to do that? We're not exactly on speaking terms with Buttersworth."

"I checked her blog. She's giving one of her tours of the Wright house tomorrow in Oak Park," Anne said, recalling that Betsy Buttersworth was on the board of preservationists for the Frank Lloyd Wright Home and Studio in Oak Park. She felt it her responsibility—no her duty—to make sure that the public was educated on Wright's Prairie Style architecture and that she should be the one educating them.

Chapter Forty-One

"C'mon, Anne, we have to go! The first tour's at 10 a.m. We're never going to make it," CC yelled out the car window to Anne. She'd pulled up at Anne's house so they could go to Oak Park for the Frank Lloyd Wright tour.

"Just a minute!" Anne held up a finger. She pulled a towel out of the back seat of her car and wrapped the fake Phoenix glass vase in it. Grabbing her large orange Prada bag, she got into the passenger seat of the car.

CC found parking on the street in front of the Frank Lloyd Wright Home and Studio. Anne jumped out of the car and flew to the courtyard which was the gathering place for tours. "I'll go get our tickets," CC said, walking up behind Anne.

CC went into the gift shop and purchased two tickets for the home and studio tour. When she came back to the courtyard, she didn't see Anne. She gazed around the small garden but there were no hiding places. Looking through the stained glass windows, she could see Anne's head bobbing along with the tour group. "Anne," she hissed through the slightly open window.

Anne gave her a look, holding her finger up to her mouth.

"Anne," CC hissed again, louder.

Anne walked out of the house. "What? I'm on the tour," Anne said.

"We're not on this tour. I've got tickets. We're at 11:15 a.m.," CC said, holding up the tickets.

Anne checked the time on her phone. 11:15? That was almost 45 minutes away. She didn't like to wait. She looked back at the tour that was heading into the house. There was definitely room. "There's room on this tour," Anne insisted.

"Anne, there will be more room on our tour. I want to be able to take pictures. I paid an extra $5."

"What do you mean?"

"You have to pay $5 extra to take pictures." She held up her wristband. "I bought you one, too."

"Bet that was Betsy's idea," Anne said, putting the wristband on.

"I'm going to the bathroom. I'll be right back," CC said, walking back to the gift shop where the bathrooms were. When she came back to the courtyard, she saw Anne's blonde head bobbing along with the Japanese tourists. For the first time, she towered over a crowd. She gave a deep sigh. "Anne," she hissed insistently.

Anne turned around with a surprised look on her face.

CC motioned for her to come back outside.

"What now?"

"It's only 11 o'clock. Look at the tickets. It's 11:15. Our tour's at 11:15."

"This one had an open space." Anne pointed back at the group that had kept moving without her.

"It doesn't matter. We paid for 11:15 and that's when our tour is." CC stopped talking when she saw the blank look on Anne's face. She just didn't get it.

When 11:15 finally arrived, Anne was the first in line. "Tickets, please." Betsy was collecting tickets from the tour group at the same time she was carrying on a conversation on her Bluetooth headset. "Hillstrom," Betsy said with a surprised look.

"Buttersworth," Anne said, passing her her ticket.

Betsy stared at it, making sure that the time was correct. "Hillstrom, you're on this tour. Go on in." Betsy clicked her headset and went back to her phone conversation.

Anne and CC shuffled by, filing into the entryway. CC took many photos of the individual details in the home as they waited for Betsy to start the tour. The room soon became crowded as their fellow ticket holders joined them.

"Wright believed that homes should live in harmony with nature, and he brought that design aesthetic to this–his first home. Every element is designed for form and function." Betsy started the tour by describing the architect's vision.

"In 1899, when Wright came to Oak Park from Chicago, he said it was because of the greenery here," Betsy continued, leading the group into the living room which featured the famous stained glass windows.

"You know, Anne, Oak Park was experiencing a growth boom during the entire 1890s," CC whispered to Anne.

"Sssh," Anne hissed loudly.

Betsy turned and gave Anne a pointed look.

Entering the dining room, she pointed out the furniture that Wright had designed. "Notice that high-backed chairs were used and scaled so that when guests would enter and exit, it created a sense of a room within a room."

They climbed the stairs to the second floor barrel-vaulted playroom where Wright's six children acted out plays on the small stage. Anne marveled at the architect's use of light. A keyboard floated in the air, its base hidden under the stairs of the balcony.

"You know, Anne, the balcony and domed roof is supported by a system of robust chains, similar to those used by St. Paul's Cathedral in London," CC said, looking up.

"That's very interesting, CC," Anne said.

Going back downstairs, they headed through the passageway that led to Wright's studio. A tree was growing up through the center of it. "In Wright's day," Betsy said, "this was a willow tree; however, when that tree died, the preservation society replaced it with a honey locust tree."

Entering the studio, CC stared up at the octagonal ceiling. Drafting tables were set up throughout the room and light poured in from sliding wood-encased windows. "This is where Wright played out his design details, collaborating with fellow architects and artisans," Betsy said.

"You know, Anne," CC said. "Oak Park has the world's largest collection of Frank Lloyd Wright designed homes."

"CC, please; I'm trying to listen," Anne whispered back to CC.

Frustrated, CC turned around and continued her conversation with the nice Japanese tourist standing behind her. "Wright was involved with every aspect of his homes. After building a home for one couple, Wright instructed the wife to wear a green dress to match the home's décor during the open house," CC whispered.

The tourist nodded politely and smiled, not understanding a word.

"This concludes the tour," Betsy said. "As President of the Preservation Society, I'd like to thank you for your donations today. Please visit our gift shop and come back soon."

After all the other tour goers filed out of the studio, Anne and CC walked up to Betsy. "Buttersworth, we need to talk to you. It's important," Anne said.

Betsy peered over Anne's shoulder to look out the window at the crowd gathering for the next tour. "The next group is starting. I don't have time for this now." She rushed past them.

"Buttersworth," Anne called after her. Betsy ignored her, and clicked on her Bluetooth headset.

"Let's do the walking tour," CC said to Anne. Entering the gift shop, they paid for the walking tour of Wright's historic Oak Park homes and picked up the recorded tour headphones. The tour took them around nine houses in downtown Oak Park, describing architectural details. Anne listened intently. CC wandered up and down and around the yards to get a closer look at the various design elements. After dropping the headsets back at the gift shop, Anne said, "My feet are tired. That was a lot of walking."

"Let's get lunch and take a break," CC said. They enjoyed lunch at Hemingway's French Bistro, an old Oak Park landmark. Anne had the ham and Gruyere crêpes and CC had the warm goat cheese salad with julienned beets and a fresh chive dressing sprinkled with last year's ghost peppers from her private reserve hidden in her white Coach purse.

Chapter Forty-Two

Anne sat at her kitchen table staring at the fake Phoenix vase. Just the fact that it was a fake was enough to irritate her. On top of that, the fact that Betsy wouldn't give her the time of day infuriated her. *Betsy came from Chicago just like the rest of us,* Anne thought. Just because she married rich and moved to Oak Park doesn't make her any better or worse than me. "If you stand on the east side of Austin Avenue in Chicago, you can toss a pebble across the street and it will land in Oak Park. It's not really that big of a deal," she said, looking up at Sassy who was perched on the shelf above the table. Sassy purred in agreement. Anne got up and looked in the fridge. Nothing there worth eating.

Anne sat back at the kitchen table and held the vase in her hands. She wasn't going to let this rest. She drove the short 20 minutes to Betsy Buttersworth's home in Oak Park, a restored Frank Lloyd Wright home on the national register. Anne had only been to the house one time before for a mutual friend's engagement party. Betsy loved to show off her money. This was much too important to worry about that.

Anne pulled into the long, narrow driveway. Betsy's periwinkle blue Aston Martin was parked in front of the detached garage. Anne was careful not to park too close to it. The landscaping was very neat but uninspiring. The showcase was the Wright home and the brass plaque that told you so, placed right above the doorbell so you couldn't miss it. Anne's temperature rose a bit glancing at the plaque.

She rang the doorbell and tapped her foot impatiently. Betsy opened it, wearing yoga pants and drinking Smart water. "Anne Hillstrom, so nice to see you. To what do I owe this pleasure?"

"Betsy, I know it's late but this is really important. I have something to show you."

In her mad dash over, Anne had forgotten that she was wearing "the pants." She didn't want to feed the fire with the flowered pants she had "taken" from Betsy, but it was too late now.

Betsy gave the pants a onceover but didn't say a word. They walked into the living room. "Sit down. Can I get you something to drink?" She looked Anne up and down. "Perhaps a Diet Coke?" She emphasized the word *Diet*.

Anne's blood started to boil but she bit her tongue. "I'm fine." Anne unwrapped the twelve-inch vase from the towel and placed it on the coffee table.

Betsy glanced at it with a disdainful look. "This is what you want to show me? A Phoenix vase?"

"Take a closer look at it," Anne urged.

Betsy lifted up the vase, twisting and turning it into the light. She examined the mark on the bottom and then placed it back down. "It's a very good copy. I recognize the pattern because I have the original."

Anne said, "Yes I know. I remember seeing you carry it at the Whitmore estate sale."

"Don't tell me you were fooled by the copy and were cheated?"

Anne restrained her temper and bit her tongue. As she counted to ten silently in her head, she noticed the alabaster Egyptian vase in the corner of the living room. Ignoring Betsy, she walked over to take a closer look. "Where'd you get this?" Anne asked.

Betsy walked over. "This is a very special piece. I bought it from Mr. Ripley."

"I don't remember seeing it at the Whitmore or Packwall sale, and those are the only ones he's held recently."

"Oh, no; this came from his private collection. He saves some of his best estate pieces for his preferred customers." Anne's puzzled look made Betsy continue. "Very pricy items. I'm afraid, Hillstrom, they'd be a bit out of your price range."

"Who are these preferred customers?"

"Not people you'd know for the most part. Some ladies from my country club, others from the Gold Coast and North Shore and even some politicians' wives. It's a very select list." Betsy waved her manicured nails. "In fact, Nancy Packwall was a preferred customer. I was a little disappointed that Mr. Ripley didn't have those pants available before the public estate sale."

Anne's temper cooled. After all, she was wearing the pants.

"What's this all about?" Betsy said.

"Nothing. I just really liked the vase and was hoping maybe you'd sell me the original."

"Where'd you get that copy anyway?"

"I got it from Banning."

"I can't believe that he'd sell you a fake," Betsy said. "My friends and I have bought many antiques from Banning. They've all been top quality. He's helped decorate many of my friends from book club's homes. Most of the customers on the preferred list have been very pleased with Banning. You know, Anne, you should be more careful. I'm sure this was a mistake."

Anne had a sour look on her face.

Betsy gave a pointed look at the pants. "I'd never sell the original vase but I would entertain a fair trade."

"I would never sell these pants." Anne made for the front door and headed to her car.

"Wait! You forgot your Phoenix vase," Betsy said in a snide tone, standing in the doorway holding the fake Phoenix glass vase like it was contagious.

Anne got out of her car, stomped back across the driveway, grabbed the vase from Betsy's hand and stormed off back to her car. She headed immediately to CC's.

Chapter Forty-Three

CC and Anne sat in the gazebo, sipping iced tea. CC wanted Anne to calm herself before getting into a conversation. Anne hyperventilated when she was worked up. "Take deep breaths, Anne; count to ten. Have a little tea. It's sun tea. I had it out all morning. I added a little sugar and mint," CC said.

As they sat, they watched the monarch butterflies floating around the milkweed. "Anne, look at the monarchs. I read somewhere a couple weeks back that the monarchs are becoming extinct in Illinois because of the shortage of milkweed plants. A lot of people think milkweed are not attractive because they're weeds. But it's where monarchs lay their eggs," CC continued. "I was amazed that days after I planted it, the monarchs came. I've seen some eggs."

Anne took a big gulp of her iced tea. "Yes, the butterflies are nice."

Bandit stormed off the deck and chased the monarchs away. They weren't as tasty as bumblebees but he had to try. He lay down next to CC, panting in the summer heat.

"So, what's going on?" CC asked.

"I went over to Buttersworth's house. I showed her the vase, and she did have the original. She also had the exact same alabaster Egyptian vase we saw at the warehouse but hers was real too." Anne talked very fast trying to catch her breath.

"Did she buy that from the Whitmore sale, too?"

"No, she bought it from Mr. Ripley at a pre-sale for the Whitmore estate. She's on a 'so-called' preferred customers list. A select la-di-da la-di-da," Anne said with a sarcastic tone. "If there are copies of all these antiques, CC, then someone has the real Paul Revere spoon."

"If they have the real spoon, why do you think they came after your fake?"

"That's what we have to find out."

"We can't go to the police. They'll ask us where we got the vase from. We can't tell them we broke into Tim Whitmore's warehouse," CC said.

"I've got an idea." Anne said.

Chapter Forty-Four

Anne stood in front of her full-length 1890s cherry wood mirror—excuse me—looking glass. She'd bought the vintage Diane von Furstenberg wrap dress a size smaller than she'd been a few weeks ago. She'd planned on fitting into it as a reward for sticking to her low-carb diet. She turned sideways to look at her profile. The wrap tugged a little at her waist and hugged her hips a little too closely. She walked to the corner of the living room and plugged in the treadmill, removing the blouses lying on the handlebars. She walked back to the looking glass and moved Sassy who was staring at her reflection. She really loved the feel of the champagne silk against her skin. She hadn't dressed for a man in many years. She took off the dress and put on a dandelion yellow sundress that was more forgiving. Anne half-twirled left and right, watching the skirt float around. Even with all her cheating she'd managed to lose eight pounds and thought she looked pretty good. She'd tried to give up the one thing most dear to a Swede's heart—butter.

She'd called Detective Towers—Nigel—and told him she wanted to return the favor and take him to her favorite restaurant, Ann Sather's. They'd arranged to meet for lunch.

Anne rushed into the storefront restaurant on Chicago's north side. She'd forgotten how difficult finding parking in the Lakeview neighborhood was. She scanned the room, looking for him. The back wall was decorated with Swedish folk dancers. Nigel was sitting at a table underneath them. Anne walked over to him. Nigel had been waiting for 20 minutes. He stood up, bumping his knee on the small wooden table. "Hello, Anne," he said.

Anne gave him a big smile. "Nigel, I'm so sorry I kept you waiting."

"Nonsense; you're right on time." He rushed around the table and held her chair out. Anne sat down and he pushed her chair in under the table.

"Have you ever been here before?" Anne asked, placing her napkin in her lap.

"No, I haven't. It's quite charming," he said.

"I've been coming here since I was a little girl, but it was open long before then. It's one of Chicago's best Swedish restaurants," Anne said. "Everything here is made from scratch. I grew up in Lakeview. It's a big Swedish community."

"I thought by your last name you were Swedish," Nigel said.

Anne nodded. "My father was a professor in Sweden and came here to teach history at North Park University. That's why I was late. When I couldn't find parking on the street, I went and parked at North Park, using my dad's parking pass."

"Oh, is your dad still teaching?"

"No. Both my parents are dead."

"Sorry to hear that," Nigel said.

"Tack Sa Mycket, thank you very much," Anne said. The waitress came over and poured Anne a cup of coffee. She refilled Nigel's cup. They placed their order.

"So, Nigel, I have to admit I have another reason for asking you to lunch," Anne said, leaning forward against the table.

Nigel smiled. "I felt something, too."

Anne gave him a quizzical look. "Oh, no, I meant I wanted to ask for your help."

Nigel's face turned bright red. "Yes, of course."

The waitress brought their order. Anne's Swedish meatballs were dripping with gravy over the hot buttered noodles. She cut a slice of the still warm limpa bread and slathered on a generous helping of creamy, sweet butter. She took a bite, closed her eyes and made a sigh of delight. Nigel turned a brighter red. "Nigel, you have to try the limpa bread. It's delicious," she said. Anne then remembered her purpose for meeting with him. "So, Nigel, I found this vase. I can't really tell you where. Wait, let me get it," She reached into her large, orange Prada bag and pulled out the fake Phoenix glass vase.

"That's beautiful," he said, looking up from his potato sausage.

"It would be if it were real," Anne said. "That's where I need your help. CC and I stumbled across the vase and a whole building full of fake replicas of all kinds of different antiques—paintings, statutes, vases, everything you can imagine."

"Anne, where is this building?" Nigel said.

"Well," she paused for a moment and decided it was best to be vague. "That's part of the problem. The building isn't there anymore."

Nigel put his fork down and gave her a harsh look. "The building disappeared?"

"It kind of burned to the ground."

"Anne, I don't think you should tell me anymore."

"We didn't burn it down," Anne said. "It's all about the spoon."

"We're back to the spoon again. Anne, you said yourself that the spoon is fake."

"That's the point. The spoon is fake. This vase is fake. Everything in the building was fake, and they were replicas of antiques sold at Tim Whitmore's estate sale."

After they had cleared their dinner plates, the waitress set down a plate with two large cinnamon rolls with white creamy icing dripping down the sides, fresh from the oven before them. Anne was momentarily diverted as she reached for one, her attention turned back to the task at hand. "We think—that is CC and I— believe that Banning, Tim Whitmore's antique dealer, murdered him because Tim found out that Banning was swindling him. He was replacing all the millions of dollars of antiques that he was purchasing on Whitmore's behalf with all these cheap imitations. Banning knew Tim wouldn't know the difference."

"Anne, after you told me about the spoon the first time, I did follow up with the Kenilworth police. There is no open homicide case for Tim Whitmore. I looked at the medical records myself. He had extensive artery blockage."

"What about Banning?" Anne asked.

"When you told me that you'd found arsenic on the spoon and someone had broken into your house to find it, I considered that Banning might be a person of interest," Nigel said. "Anne, he checks out; he has no criminal record. He's a well-respected businessman."

"But, Nigel. . ."

He interrupted her. "That's enough. You have to stop this obsessing about the spoon."

Anne took a bite of her cinnamon roll in silence. Its taste wasn't quite so sweet anymore.

Chapter Forty-Five

The road to Lake Geneva, Wisconsin, was a short drive over the Illinois border. At this time of year, it was packed with summer tourists. The beautiful lake was surrounded by luxury resorts and multimillion-dollar vacation homes. One of them was for sale. That's where CC and Anne were headed—the Kirby estate. Brian Kirby was a wealthy banker. When all the savings and loans in Chicago had gone belly up in the 1980s, Brian had gotten out when the getting was good. He'd sold his 80 brick and mortars to a national bank. His 20,000 square-foot Italian-style villa was nestled on a bluff overlooking the deep, crystal blue waters of one of Wisconsin's largest lakes. Anne had learned from Buttersworth that Mr. Ripley was holding a preferred customer presale for the estate over the weekend.

Mr. Ripley looked dapper as always in his gray summer-weight Armani suit, accented with a white carnation in the lapel. "Excuse me, ladies," he said to Anne and CC as they walked toward the front door. "This sale is invitation only. I didn't see your names on my list." He checked the clipboard in his hand.

"Mr. Ripley, we really need to talk to you about something important," CC said.

He hesitated. "Since you are valued customers, why don't you come in and look around? We can talk when I have a free moment."

"Yes, yes, definitely, we will," Anne said, impatient to get inside.

"Stay focused," CC whispered as they walked through the double-arched doors. A stained glass chandelier dangled down, illuminating the Italian travertine floors. The foyer was dripping with gold, including gold-leafed wallpaper. Tuscany colors were everywhere. A round marble table stood center stage in the middle of the foyer. Anne stopped to admire it. Instead of flowers, a large gold cherub was holding court on its surface. The foyer exited through 30-foot high roman pillars into a great room which had floor to ceiling sliding windows overlooking the lake. A large marble fireplace and white Italian leather furniture decorated the room. CC went to sit on the veranda.

"I'm going to look around a little bit," Anne said. After the living room, she wandered through the kitchen, admiring the copper pots and pans hanging over the large quartz island. The huge dining room shared the same passion for gold and gilt as the entryway. A small door led off the dining room. Anne entered an office. On the wall were pictures of Cragin Bank, the first savings and loan that Kirby had acquired in Chicago. There were pictures of corporate outings, Brian with Mayor Richard J. Daley, a framed diploma from Yale and a young Brian Kirby on the Yale swim team dated 1963. On the wall behind the desk were family photos and boating pictures. It was a lifetime up on the wall. Now he was gone and the pictures hung silent, like a ghost in the corner.

Anne sat down at the desk trying to estimate its size to see if it would fit through her door. Of course, the hundred-year-old oak carved desk was twice as wide as her front door but she still tried to do the math. She peeked out through the French doors and saw CC sitting with Mr. Ripley on the veranda.

CC sat on the veranda, waiting for Mr. Ripley, enjoying her freshly brewed espresso and Italian butter cookies. A 30-foot sailboat drifted by. She thought about Tony and the day on his boat and their time in the garden. Everywhere she looked she was reminded of him. She wondered if this was what it felt like to live in Italy. A shadow loomed in front of her. "I have a minute now if you wish to talk," Mr. Ripley said.

CC hadn't noticed his accent before. Surprising because normally she had a very good ear for accents. It was a slight accent that she could tell he tried not to reveal. It sounded eastern European. "Mr. Ripley, thank you, yes."

He sat down across from CC. He motioned to the server who brought over a tea service and set it down in front of him. He waved the server off. "May I pour you some tea?"

"No, thank you, I'm having coffee." CC held up the cup on the table in front of her.

Mr. Ripley reached into his pocket and pulled out a small envelope containing tealeaves. He placed them in a metal mesh tea ball and poured the hot water through the ball. He took the sugar tongs and pulled out a single sugar cube. He put the sugar cube in his mouth and sipped the tea through it, oblivious to CC's intent gaze.

She watched the whole ritual. *Not Slavic, Russian,* CC thought. She'd spent time in the steel mills in the Vologda region of Russia, just outside of the Ukraine. Sipping tea through sugar cubes was a Russian custom. "This is a beautiful home. The view of the lake is gorgeous," she said to Mr. Ripley.

"Mr. Kirby loved the water. He had several homes but this was his favorite. That's his boat." Ripley pointed toward the dock where a wooden Chris-craft was docked—battered—a sizeable hole in the front of its hull.

"What happened there?" CC asked.

"He got caught in a storm on the lake. The boat was recovered, but he was never found. It's very sad. He really loved the water."

"Is the boat for sale? I know someone who might be interested."

Anne walked out onto the veranda to join them, her arms overflowing. "CC, you're not going to believe. . ."

"Anne, Mr. Ripley is ready to talk to us now," CC said.

Anne plopped down onto the open chair next to CC. She pulled the vase out of her large orange Prada bag. She handed the vase to Mr. Ripley who looked it over for a moment.

"Is good imitation. What does it have to do with me?" he asked.

"Betsy Buttersworth bought the real vase that looked just like this one at the Whitmore estate sale. She also bought an alabaster Egyptian vase."

"Yes, I remember selling that to Mrs. Buttersworth," he interrupted. "She has very good taste."

"We found replicas of many of Mr. Whitmore's antiques at a warehouse owned by him," CC said.

"I still don't know what this has to do with me," Mr. Ripley said.

Anne pulled out the spoon and held it up with a flourish. "This is the silver spoon that Banning is looking for. We believe that Banning was buying millions of dollars worth of antiques for Tim Whitmore and replacing them with fakes," Anne said.

"I know nothing about this. Everything that I bought or sold from the Whitmore estate was authentic. I have the provenance on all the items. Banning is a very reputable buyer and refers me to many of his clients. Take a look around. Mr. Kirby was a long-time client of Banning's. In fact, he brokered the purchase of the Chris-craft boat."

"Mr. Ripley, we intend on exposing Banning as a embezzler," CC said. "This could impact your reputation."

"Why don't you go to the police?"

CC and Anne looked at each other. "They didn't believe us."

"How do you want me to help you?" Mr. Ripley asked.

"You can tell Banning that we bought the spoon by mistake for five dollars. We know it's worth a lot more money. We're willing to sell it back to him for the right price," CC said.

"I think you should call him yourself directly. I don't want to be involved. I have a reputation to protect," said Mr. Ripley. He stood up, put his tea back in his pocket. "Good day, ladies." He walked back into the house, closing the French door with a loud click.

Anne and CC looked at each other again. It had never occurred to them to call Banning themselves.

Driving down Route 14 on the way home, Anne screamed, "CC, look! An antique store!" They'd just entered the small town of Richmond, Illinois. Anne was pointing at a large two-story Victorian painted lady that held a sign reading *Emporium* in large yellow letters. "Can we stop?"

CC parked in the front of the building. They walked into the old home that had been transformed into an antique hunter's dream. Shelves were overflowing with teacups, vases, silverware and all sorts of knick-knacks. Pictures and paintings hung haphazardly on the wall.

"This is great." Anne smelled bargains in the dusty, crowded store. She picked up a silver decorative monkey, picturing it on her mantle.

CC browsed selectively and made her way through the myriad of rooms at a much quicker pace than Anne.

Little interested her but she did find a birdhouse crafted from tin that she had to have for her garden.

Anne hovered over a long glass-front case, eyeing the display of vintage jewelry, admiring the amber bead necklace, delicate cameo pins, and marcasite rings. She was struck by the chunky amber necklace and strained to see a price on it. The price tag was hidden from view, a pet peeve of Anne's. She didn't like wasting time finding someone to tell her how much something cost. She punished shop owners by leaving and never returning. In Anne's world of antiquing, it was a capital offense.

CC stepped up behind Anne, gazing into the case. "See anything?" she asked.

"I was looking at that necklace," Anne said, pointing at the butterscotch amber necklace.

"It's pretty," CC said.

"Yes, but I can't see the price."

"Let's find someone to help," CC said.

"It's too late now. I've lost interest."

CC added another *Anne-syncrasie* to the running list in her head, right after her time management skills and her distorted view of finance.

Anne walked to the front desk where she paid for the monkey and a pair of lapis lazuli earrings. Placing their purchases in the car, they walked the few storefronts to the old-fashioned drug store that also had a lunch counter. They opted to sit at the counter on the tall red vinyl stools instead of waiting for a table. They both ordered Green River floats and grilled cheese sandwiches.

While they waited for their order, Anne wandered around, investigating the novelty items and jars of penny candies. They had all Anne's favorites from when she was a little girl, like bulls eyes, wax juice bottles, pixie straws, licorice pipes and dots on the paper. She filled a bag with a selection of all of them.

She stopped to test the hand cream made locally by a beekeeper. She walked past the penny scale that told your fortune. She knew her fortune would be bad if she stood on the scale after going off her diet the last few days. On the back wall were hickory walking sticks, old-fashioned crutches and a vintage wheelchair made out of wicker. Everything had a price tag dangling from it.

"Anne, the food's here!" CC called over to her.

Anne hurried back and sat on the stool next to CC, swiveling back and forth on the seat. She was very excited about moving on to the next antique store. CC took a bite and sighed, "This is so good, Anne, It's Gruyere, cheddar and Swiss. It's full of gooey goodness."

"They've got some really incredible antique medical supplies. I saw a leather doctor's bag. It had to be from the 1800s," Anne said.

They finished their lunch. Anne swiveled facing CC. "What's the plan?"

"We contact Banning and let him know we have the spoon and it's for sale," CC said.

"Sounds good. Can we stop at the other little shop I saw on the way out of town?"

CC sighed, exasperated. "Okay, but only for a few minutes." They paid for their lunch and walked onto the next shop.

Chapter Forty-Six

Anne set the video camera on top of the refrigerator in her kitchen. She looked through the viewfinder to make sure it was the perfect angle to see CC sitting at the table. She placed an art deco silver napkin holder in front of it. "All set," she said to CC.

The doorbell rang. They looked at each other. "Are we really going to do this?" Anne asked.

CC nodded at her. They answered the door together. Banning stood straight-faced on the other side, holding a briefcase. He didn't say a word.

"Mr. Banning, please come in," CC said.

He followed her into the kitchen. Banning sat down at the table and placed the briefcase next to him on the floor. From above, Sassy uttered a low growl, her tail rocking like a pendulum. She looked like a Kit-Cat clock perched on the shelf.

"I understand that you were mistakenly sold a very expensive spoon," Banning said.

"Yes, Paul Revere's Midnight Ride spoon," Anne said.

"May I see it?" Banning asked.

Anne took the spoon out of her large orange Prada bag, unwrapped it from the cotton cloth and handed it to Banning.

He took out an eye loupe and looked the spoon over carefully. "How did you know what the spoon was?"

"We're antique hunters. We know a great deal about history and artifacts. This is a very important spoon. It belongs in a museum," CC said.

Anne gave her a sharp look.

"It holds a lot of sentimental value to the Whitmore family. They were very upset when they learned it was sold by mistake. They have authorized me to offer you $5,000 cash for the spoon." He lifted his briefcase, snapped it open. With the top of the case facing the two women, he pulled out a stack of twenties still wrapped in a Federal Reserve band. He closed the briefcase, put it on the floor and placed the stack in the middle of the table waiting for a response.

Anne got very excited. CC slowly pushed the stack of money back to Banning's side of the table. "It's worth ten times that," she said.

Banning lifted up his briefcase again and pulled out another stack. He placed it on top of the other, pushing it toward CC's side of the table. "$10,000 is as much as I'm allowed to go."

CC reached under the table and pulled out the imitation Phoenix vase and placed it next to the money. "How much would you give me for this vase?"

Banning's expression turned ashen. "Where'd you get that?" he asked in a loud voice.

"From Tim Whitmore's warehouse."

"What is this?" he stammered. "You know the spoon is fake, don't you? Are you trying to blackmail me?"

"We know that you were buying millions of dollars of antiques for Mr. Whitmore and replacing them with replicas," CC said.

"We know your plan," Anne added.

He reached into his briefcase and pulled out another stack of twenties. "Here, $15,000. Keep your mouths shut."

"We're antique hunters. We can't be bought," Anne said. "You're a disgrace to antique lovers."

Banning pounded the table. He grabbed the cash and stood up. Anne grabbed the spoon off the table and backed up against the sink counter, terrified. This time, Banning opened the briefcase and pulled out a gun. "All I want is the spoon. I don't want to hurt anyone."

"What about Tim Whitmore?"

"What about Tim? The fat slob died of a heart attack. What do you expect after eating all that fried hillbilly food," Banning said, waving the gun around. "He didn't have a clue that the antiques weren't real. His idea of class was his framed autographed poster of Richard Petty."

As CC and Banning spoke, Anne felt Sassy's piercing stare. Over Banning's head, Sassy arched her back, preparing to pounce at the sound of the can opener. Anne reached behind herself and pushed the lever down. The noise was startling.

Banning's surprised look turned to terror when a 30-pound brass coffee grinder and a 20-pound Persian cat both landed on his head. He fell to the ground, knocked out cold.

Anne ran to a kitchen drawer and pulled out a roll of packing tape. Quickly, she and CC sealed Banning up into a cocoon. Anne then called Detective Towers who showed up a short while later.

"Okay, ladies, I'm sure there's a very good explanation for all this. You said you caught the man who broke into your house. I take it this is him." He looked down at Banning still tied up on the floor.

Banning tried to talk through the tape covering his mouth. Detective Towers peeled back the tape over Banning's mouth. "These women are crazy!" Banning cried. "They called me over to look at an antique they wanted to sell. Next thing I know, they're robbing me!"

Anne took out the stepstool, climbed up and took the video camera off the the top of the fridge. "That's not true. We have proof." Anne played back the whole scene for Detective Towers.

"You bi. . . ."

Before the *b* word could come out of Banning's mouth, Nigel put the tape back over it. "Ladies, I have to say I was wrong."

Anne then brought out the tea leaves. "These tea leaves are laced with arsenic. They were in the same bag with the spoon that Banning used to poison Tim Whitmore."

Banning screamed something undecipherable through the tape. Nigel ripped it off again, along with a little bit of skin. "Okay; I'll admit I stole from Whitmore. But I didn't killed him! Why would I kill him? He was my golden goose!" Banning protested.

"Because he found out that you were charging him millions of dollars for cheap fakes," CC said.

"He never knew. After he died, I was afraid that I might get caught, so I got rid of all the fakes except for that damn spoon. They were supposed to only sell the real antiques at the estate sale," Banning said.

"How do you explain the warehouse?"

Banning grew quiet. "I want to call my attorney."

Detective Towers cut the packing tape off completely and put Banning in handcuffs. "We can arrange for that," he said. Detective Towers called for a squad car to take Banning. Two police officers came to the door and took him away. "I'll need to take the spoon for evidence," Detective Towers said.

Anne held onto the spoon. She was reluctant to let it go. CC nudged her shoulder. "I'll make sure you get it back," Detective Towers said.

Anne smiled at the thought of seeing Detective Towers again and handed him the spoon. For the first time since all the excitement had started, she noticed that his tie matched her pants. She wondered if it was a coincidence.

After Detective Towers left, Anne said, "I never showed you what I got from the Kirby sale." She reached into her large orange Prada bag and pulled out a small glass case.

CC eyed the case.

"They're commemorative stamps from the 1964 summer Olympics in Tokyo. They were only sold during the Olympics. I'm going to frame them and put them in my bathroom," Anne said. "Neat, huh?"

"Yeah."

"He had a lot of items from the 1964 Olympics in his office. He also had a lot of Japanese vases but this was all I could afford."

"It's funny because the rest of the house was very Italian," CC said.

Chapter Forty-Seven

Tony stood behind CC, holding his hands over hers as she struggled with the steering wheel of the Biagletti. The waves were slapping against the boat's hull, and the wind was gusting, pushing them across Lake Michigan. She could feel his chest pressing up against her back and his heart beating.

They docked the boat at Saginaw, Michigan, and walked along the pier, which was adjacent to quaint shops that nestled along it. Settling on the Captain's Table restaurant, they sat on the outdoor deck overlooking the lake. They watched the sailboats drift by, white sails billowing in the wind.

"I've always wanted to race in the Mackinac run. I worked on one of the race sailboats for the Chicago Yacht Club," he said.

"How come you never have?"

"The crew is usually reserved for club members and the Yachting elite. I'm more the hired help."

"The Biagletti is beautiful. You're an artist." She paused. "That reminds me. I know of a boat that you might be interested in. I saw it at an estate sale in Lake Geneva. It's a 1932 Chris-Craft wooden powerboat. It's in pretty bad shape, but it's a great boat. I think you could get a good deal on it."

Chapter Forty-Eight

Anne thumbed through the racks of clothes in Nancy Packwall's closet, hoping for another find like her flowered pants. Everything was pretty much picked over from the first sale. Betsy Buttersworth hadn't even bothered to show up for this second sale. Anne held up a sleeveless beaded tank top and looked for a place to try it on. She closed the closet doors and slipped it on. *Not quite right*, she thought, as the top barely slid over her hips.

Where has Anne gone off to? CC asked herself as she walked through the main floor of the house. She wasn't so much interested in the sale, as she wanted to find Mr. Ripley to tell him about Banning. She didn't see him anywhere. She stepped out into the backyard for a cigarette. She didn't want Anne to see that she was smoking again. All the stress of the Banning adventure had her unnerved. She wandered through the garden. The royal raindrop crabapple tree spread its arms across the yard, wind chimes and birdhouses danced in the trees' limbs. She sat down on the circular teak bench that surrounded the tree trunk. The yard had not been tended to since Nancy's death. She could tell that Nancy had loved her garden. CC finished her cigarette and followed the stepping-stones through the meadow sage. She watched the monarch butterflies land and take off on the purple landing strip. She followed the dry riverbed that was lined with yellow tickseed. She bent down to pull some weeds, including a sticker bush which pricked her finger.

When she stood up, she noticed the greenhouse. She could probably find a pair of gloves in there. Last time, the door had been locked; now it opened with a slight tug. The aroma of peat moss, manure, mushroom compost and soil filled her nostrils. To her, it was a fragrant perfume. Then she smelled the orchids. She closed her eyes and breathed deeply. Following the scent, she took in the heady aroma of hyacinth. It was coming from the Zygopetalum orchid, a variety known for its particular scent. She wondered if the plants were for sale, but caring for orchids had never been her forte. On the garden cart next to the orchids was a metal water mister. It looked like the one Marlon Brando had used in *The Godfather*.

CC admired the craftsmanship and simplicity of it. It was just what she needed. Carrying it back to the house, she went to look for Anne. She found her in the kitchen admiring a Fireking Jadeite bowl. "Are you ready to go?" CC asked.

"CC, I think this is like the bowl that's on our list," Anne said.

They looked over the list, checked the bowl and agreed that the price was right. They went to the long table in the living room to pay for their purchases. CC put the sprayer in a large brown bag. After leaving the house, they went to the car and loaded up the trunk. Anne got into the passenger side.

As CC was about to get in the car, she noticed Mr. Ripley's silver Bentley pulling into the driveway. She ran up to the car as he was getting out. "Mr. Ripley!" she called.

Mr. Ripley smiled his congenial smile.

"I wanted to let you know that the police arrested Banning. He's safely behind bars," CC said.

"I'm disappointed to learn that Banning is a thief, but I'm glad to hear he was brought to justice," Mr.

Ripley said. "Mr. Whitmore was a very nice man and had a wonderful collection." With an Eastern European flair, Ripley nodded his head, bowed and kissed her hand. "What an unusual perfume!"

CC gave him an enigmatic smile.

When they got home, CC took the mister into the backyard, anxious to try it on her pepper plants. She thought about Vito Corleone chasing his grandson around the tomato plants with a slice of orange in his mouth. She pulled the plunger back and misted the peppers. The water smelled sweet like overripe bananas. She continued spraying, just to empty it out. The first honeybee struck her in the back of the neck. She turned and screamed. Two other bees stung her arms. She dropped the mister and ran up the back stairs into the kitchen swatting madly in the air.

"What's wrong, CC?" Anne asked, sticking her head out from the refrigerator.

"Bees! I must have disturbed a hive. They're swarming all over me!"

Anne looked out the back window. She could see what looked like an entire hive of bees around the mister, some crashing into it. "What were you spraying back there?"

"I thought it was just water. I don't know. It was whatever Nancy Packwall used on her plants. I figured she had a beautiful garden so she must have known how to take care of the plants, but it smelled like ripe bananas."

"Ripe bananas?" Anne asked with a furrowed brow.

The two watched out the kitchen window for some time after the bees had subsided. Anne took one of CC's scarves and made a beekeeper's babushka. She grabbed two oven mitts. She ran quickly outside and grabbed the mister and brought it back into the kitchen.

She put it into the sink. "I can smell the bananas. It smells rotten," Anne said, sniffing.

CC brought her a small mason jar. Anne unlatched the cap on the canister and poured some of the mixture into the jar. "I'm going to take this into work with me tomorrow and see what the deal is," Anne said, putting the Mason jar into her large orange Prada bag.

Chapter Forty-Nine

Anne took the Mason jar out of her large orange Prada bag. With a syringe, she extracted a sample and put it into the VIS/NIR spectrometer. The results came back instantly, displaying a mixture of isopentyl acetate, butyl acetate, 1-hexanol, n-butanol, 1-octanol, hexyl acetate, octyl acetate, n-pentyl acetate and 2-nonanol. She put the results in her chemical database looking to match the components. "Honeybee alarm pheromone," she read. "Alarm pheromones are released when a bee stings another animal and attract other bees to the location, causing them to attack and sting the source of the threat."

"Ohmigod!" she said. She speed dialed CC. "The stuff from the mister mimics honeybee alarm pheromone."

"No wonder the bees went crazy," CC said. "Why would Nancy Packwall have honeybee alarm pheromone in a water mister?" CC flipped open her laptop and Googled *Nancy Packwall*. "There's a story in *Variety*, Anne. She died at age 70 of anaphylactic shock. She was allergic to bees. She was stung by a bee and didn't have an EpiPen on her at the time."

"Ohmigod! Banning killed Nancy Packwall, too!" Anne said.

Anne hung up with CC, grabbed the test results and the Mason jar. She drove to the police station. The desk sergeant cradled a phone receiver in his ear and held up one finger, instructing Anne to be patient. He turned his back to her, sipped his coffee and nodded his head to the voice on the other end of the phone. Anne was losing patience. When the sergeant got off the phone, Anne was a bit curt. "I need to see Detective Towers right now!" she demanded.

"Excuse me, ma'am, who are you?" the sergeant asked.

"I'm Anne Hillstrom. I have information for him about a case he's working on."

The sergeant said, "I can see if Detective Towers is in." He picked up the phone and turned his back to Anne again. She strummed her fingers on the top of the desk; this was getting very old. The sergeant hung up the phone. "Detective Towers will be down in a minute. Have a seat over there." He pointed at the wooden bench that flanked the wall.

Anne sat down, watching the schoolhouse clock tick away and police officers come and go. Some had bad guys in tow; others were on their way out to catch bad guys. She started biting her nails, a habit she'd broken and then unbroken with all the stress of their recent adventures. She was just thankful that CC hadn't started smoking again. She wouldn't let her know about the nail biting or she'd get an earful.

"Anne." Detective Towers walked up to her. His warm smile cooled Anne's temper. She stopped biting her nails and hid her hand behind her back.

"Nigel." She stood up.

"Is there someplace we can talk? Somewhere not quite so open?" Anne looked around, trying to make sure no one was listening.

"Certainly, come with me." Nigel led her up the stairs to the second floor. "We can talk in here." He walked into a small room with a wood table and a couple hard wood chairs. "Can I get you anything? A cup of coffee?"

"No, I'm fine."

"Please, sit down," he said, holding her chair out.

"I want to thank you again for your help with arresting Banning," she said.

"I'm sorry that I didn't believe you," he said, sitting across from her.

"That's okay. That's not why I'm here." She took a deep breath. "Where do I start?" She reached into her large orange Prada bag, pulled out the Mason jar and the lab results. "CC and I were at another sale at Nancy Packwall's house the other day and CC bought this lovely garden mister, an old-fashioned metal one with a pump handle. I thought she got a great deal."

Nigel smiled patiently, waiting for the point to come around.

"CC brought it home, was misting her pepper plants when she was attacked by a swarm of honeybees. She ran into the kitchen and we both watched through the window as the bees attacked the mister. Of course, as you can imagine, I wanted to know what was in that mister that upset the bees. Here's what I found." She pushed the paper across the table toward him. "I ran a chemical analysis."

Nigel read silently, moving his lips and then looked at Anne. "What is this?"

"It mimics honeybee alarm pheromone. A bee emits this when it's in danger. It drives the other bees crazy. Nancy Packwall died of anaphylactic shock. She was allergic to bees. I think Banning killed Nancy Packwall, too."

"Where's the connection? If he killed Whitmore, which we're not even sure of yet, it was probably because Whitmore discovered that Banning was stealing from him. As far as I know, Banning had no relationship with Nancy Packwall."

"I saw him at the first estate sale at her house. He must have known her."

The revelation struck Nigel. "Banning's out on bail," Nigel said, grabbing his gun. "I'll find him." His warm expression turned suddenly cold. He glanced at the clock. "I'll call you."

Chapter Fifty

CC and Tony met John Hayward, the groundskeeper at the Kirby estate. He led them to the boat. "Mr. Kirby loved this boat. He had it restored. Shame what happened. It was a terrible thing. He was a good man. Feel free to look at the boat. I'll be up at the rose garden if you have any questions."

"Thanks," CC said as Hayward walked away.

Tony walked around the boat, touching the wood. "She's a beauty all right," he said. He crawled under the dry docked powerboat to look at the keel. "The structure's in good shape." He examined the two-foot hole. "You said that Mr. Kirby hit some rocks during a storm on the lake."

"I believe that's what I heard happened."

"That doesn't make sense because Lake Geneva's one of the deepest lakes in the area. It's hundreds of feet deep so there aren't any rocks offshore. Also, this hole isn't very jagged. It almost looks like someone knocked the planks out with a hammer. There's no splinters; run your hand along the edge here." Tony pointed to the hole in the boat's hull.

CC obliged him. "It's smooth." She stood back and looked at the boat.

A short while later, CC sat in the passenger side of Tony's car—a white F100 as Tony drove and fiddled with the radio. She gave out a big yawn and popped her eyes open quickly trying not to fall asleep.

Out of the corner of his eye, Tony caught her. "It's okay. You can close your eyes. It's been a long day. We have a little drive ahead of us."

"Are you sure? I feel bad. I wanted to keep you company," she said, holding back another yawn.

"You get some rest." He smiled at her. He turned the radio off and kept his eyes on the road. The whine of the engine and the monotonous scenery lulled CC to sleep. She dreamed she was swimming on Oak Street Beach. The waves kept pulling her further and further away from the shore; the harder she struggled, the more the beach disappeared from view until she was floating on her back looking up at the sky.

The truck suddenly squealed to a stop, waking CC up with a start. She'd fallen asleep on Tony's shoulder. With a foggy head, she remembered something about swimming. She looked out the passenger window and noticed that they were in front of her house.

"Do you want to come in?" CC asked, reaching for the door handle.

"I'd love to, but I have an early morning and a long ride. Thank you for showing me the boat."

CC couldn't wait any longer. She leaned in and gave him a quick kiss on the cheek. Tony took her face in his hands and kissed her on the lips. CC smiled and flew out of the car like a teenage girl on prom night. She watched Tony drive off. As the tail lights faded, she said, "I know. Brian Kirby was an Olympic swimmer."

Chapter Fifty-One

"We haven't found Banning yet," Detective Towers said as he poured Anne a fresh glass of wine. He'd invited her to dinner at the Italian Village restaurant in downtown Chicago.

"Should I be worried? Is he going to come after me?" Anne replied.

"Anne, I don't believe he killed anyone. He's a thief but not a murderer," Nigel said. "Both Whitmore and Packwall are not homicide cases."

"What about the honeybee alarm pheromone and the arsenic on the spoon?"

"Anne, if it puts your mind at ease, I'll have both of them analyzed by our lab, but I have to give everything to homicide."

"Thank you so much." She reached across the table, took his hand and gave it a squeeze.

The waiter came over and placed a garden salad in front of Anne. Her latest diet was the paleo, which meant sticking to plants and animals that cavemen would have eaten, and avoiding dairy, grains, and processed oil and sugar. She'd been on it for a few weeks and was already sick of salads. She'd eat a caveman if she could spread butter on him.

The waiter then placed a large appetizer plate filled with fried calamari, chicken fingers and potato skins in front of Nigel. Anne's mouth started to drool as she eyed the potato skins. Nigel put a potato skin on his plate and smothered it in butter and sour cream. "I'm sorry, Anne, would you like some?" Nigel pushed the appetizer plate to her.

"I wouldn't mind one potato skin," Anne said. After Anne and Nigel finished off the appetizers, the waiter brought over two cedar plank grilled salmon entrees.

"Anne, how's your friend, CC?"

"She's fine. She's actually with her new—I don't know if you could call him her boyfriend—her friend Tony," Anne said. "He's an interesting guy. He's a shipwright. He restores vintage wooden yachts, lived in Italy or something. He's a nice enough guy."

"That sounds interesting," Nigel said, his mouth full of calamari.

"In fact, they were in Lake Geneva looking at an old powerboat or something. She and I had gone up there earlier for a preferred customer presale."

Nigel finished swallowing his large bite of salmon. "Excuse me. A what?"

"Mr. Ripley, who held the Whitmore estate sale, occasionally has a presale for preferred customers. Select customers. A friend of ours, Betsy, told us about the sale. We went up to take a look around," Anne said.

"Are you on the list?"

"No, it's more Chicago's hoity-toity, North Shore. Tim Whitmore was on it and Nancy Packwall was on it." She put her fork down. "And Brian Kirby was on it."

"Brian Kirby?"

"He owned the mansion we went to in Lake Geneva." Anne believed Nigel knew his job and knew it well. If he believed Banning didn't kill Tim Whitmore, then he didn't. She dismissed the thoughts that were creeping into her head. They split a slice of peanut butter chocolate cake. Anne didn't even bother checking her *Fitness Pal* app to see how many carbs it was. She knew she was probably already in triple digits.

Nigel paid the check and walked Anne to her car. He hunched over her with his polite question mark stance. She just loved his accent and he was wearing that tie that matched her pants. It had to be intentional.

"Nigel, I had a nice time," she said, opening her car door.

"Anne, it was lovely. I hope we can go out again sometime."

Anne blushed a bit. "I think that would be really nice."

He leaned down a bit further, kissed her on the cheek. Anne grabbed Nigel by his bony face and kissed him hard on the lips. He smiled and then held the car door open as she got in. He watched her drive off, arching his back and stretching.

Chapter Fifty-Two

When she pulled up in front of her house, CC was sitting in her car, smoking. She caught a glimpse of Anne in her rearview mirror. She put the cigarette out in the ashtray but it was too late. She waved the smoke away with her hand but she was caught.

Anne stuck her head in the window. "Don't bother CC, I saw you. When did this start again?"

"You know it's been pretty stressful. It's the first one I've had in a year."

Anne gave her a disapproving look. "How was your date?" CC asked.

"It wasn't really a date. Nigel just wanted to update me on the Banning investigation."

"What did he say?" CC followed Anne into the house.

"He hasn't found Banning yet. But the police are still convinced that Packwall and Whitmore died of natural causes"

"I can't believe it." CC sat at the kitchen table as Anne pulled the Sherlock Holmes teapot out and filled it with water.

"He said the cases are closed. There's nothing that would cause them to reopen them."

"I don't know, Anne, things just aren't adding up. Tony looked over the Kirby boat and he believes that the ship never hit rocks. The hole was manmade. Someone tampered with it."

"Why would someone do that?" Anne poured the steaming tea into two cups and set one in front of CC.

"They said they never found Kirby's body. They just assumed he drowned when they found the boat washed up on shore." CC stirred some sugar in her tea.

"That's strange because Mr. Ripley said Kirby loved the water. His Lake Geneva house was his favorite," CC said.

"There was a picture in his study of him on the 1963 Yale swim team," Anne said.

CC reached for her iPhone. As she typed, she said, "You bought the 1964 Olympic stamps there, right?"

"Yes, I showed them to you."

She flipped the phone around to show Anne. It was a picture of the 1964 US Olympic swim team, one of the names in the caption was Brian Kirby. Anne and CC looked at each other. "Even in a bad storm, I believe he'd be able to swim to shore," CC said.

"When I was talking to Nigel," Anne said. "I realized that Whitmore, Packwall and Kirby all were clients of Banning's."

"That's it!" CC said. "That's the connection."

"Betsy's on that list, too. Banning could be after her!" Anne said. She pulled her cell phone out and dialed Betsy Buttersworth. The phone went straight to voicemail. She tried a couple more times with the same result. She looked worried. "That's not like Buttersworth. That phone is always glued to her ear."

"Let's take a ride," CC said, getting up.

When they pulled up to Betsy's house, it was late. *It was too important not to wake Betsy,* Anne thought. Anne looked at CC. "Hurry!' she said, trying to call Betsy again.

Anne rang the doorbell. They could hear movement inside the house. "She probably looked out the window, saw it was you and is hiding," CC whispered behind her.

"Be quiet," Anne whispered back, knocking on the door. There was no answer. "Betsy's probably still upset with me about the vase." Anne tried the door again and it opened. The house was dark except for a glimmer coming from down the hallway.

"What are you doing?" CC hissed.

"She's obviously home." Anne and CC walked into the foyer. Anne's phone vibrated and she showed CC the text message from Nigel, "We arrested Banning, and he was carrying the authentic spoon."

"Great! Betsy's safe. We can go now before we wake her." CC grabbed Anne's arm and pulled her toward the door.

From down the hallway, they heard a chair scraping along the floor. Anne turned around. "We don't want to scare her. Let's tell her it's us. Betsy!" Anne called out, "It's Anne!"

Anne tiptoed down the hallway, followed by CC. Entering the kitchen, Betsy was sitting motionless, her face illuminated by the full moon shining through the skylight. Her eyes were wide. "Betsy, what's wrong?" Anne asked.

Betsy didn't answer, her hands remained folded in her lap. From behind the shadows, Mr. Ripley stepped out, holding a hypodermic needle. He grabbed Betsy by the hair and put the needle to her throat. Anne screamed. CC grabbed her arm.

Anne stifled her scream. Mr. Ripley said, "One word and I stick her. This needle is filled with ricin."

"I remember seeing castor bean plants in Nancy Packwall's garden. I didn't think anything of it," CC said. She turned to Anne. "Anne, ricin is a deadly poison which is made from the castor bean seed."

"Not now," Anne squeaked.

"Very good," Mr. Ripley said. "You know your poisons."

"And you know yours," CC replied. "It's not a Russian accent, is it? It's Bulgarian."

Mr. Ripley relaxed his grip a bit.

"You had me fooled with the whole Russian drinking tea through the sugar cube routine."

"That's right; I'm Bulgarian."

"Ricin is the weapon of choice for the Bulgarian secret police. It's undetectable in autopsies," CC said.

"Not now," Anne said with barely enough wind to get the words out.

"Very good again," Mr. Ripley said.

"Why? Why are you doing this?"

"It's not hard to understand. It's just about the money. I sell all these rich people overpriced antiques and then they all go on the list. When I need more money, I kill them and sell their stuff again. More rich people buy it." He waved the needle at the other two chairs. "Now you two sit down."

Anne and CC pulled out the kitchen chairs and sat in front of Betsy who was too terrified to speak. She closed her eyes and waited for the needle to plunge into her throat. "You know," Mr. Ripley said. "I should have killed you that day when you bought the pants. They're hideous. You should die just for wearing them. And you!" He looked at CC. "That perfume I smelled was hyacinth. You were in the greenhouse, weren't you that day?"

CC nodded her head.

Mr. Ripley laughed, continuing. "You've saved me lots of trouble, haven't you? It all ends here tonight." He put the needle back against Betsy's throat.

The whole time Mr. Ripley was enjoying his triumph, CC was desperately trying to reach into her purse behind her. "Yes, that's right, I was in the greenhouse. We know about the water mister. Pretty clever filling it with the alarm pheromones."

"I thought that was very clever."

Her purse snapped open. She had to keep him talking. "But what about Brian Kirby?"

"Mr. Kirby. He was very rich. He loved that boat. He wanted to take me for a ride and show it off."

CC stretched her fingers as far as she could. She could feel the top of the glass jar. "He was an Olympic swimmer. He could have easily swum across the lake."

"It's hard to swim with lead weights tied round your ankles."

CC took her index and middle fingers and desperately tried to twist the top of the jar open. "How did you know Tim Whitmore would drink the arsenic-laced tea leaves?"

"Who do you think sold him all the antique guns and uniforms?"

The lid wouldn't open.

Mr. Ripley pulled a nine-millimeter gun out of his Armani suit. He pointed it at Anne. "And you, that brooch! That was worth hundreds of thousands of dollars. And you buried it with that crazy old lady. If she would have given me the brooch in the first place, she'd still be alive."

"How are you going to explain a bullet? Everyone else you killed, you made look like an accident or natural causes. I don't think a nine-millimeter bullet is very natural, do you?" CC said. Anne sat in shock over the revelation about Sybil.

He laughed. "I like you. I'm going to kill you last."

The lid popped off the jar. With a single motion, CC tossed the hot ghost pepper powder in Mr. Ripley's face. He dropped the gun and needle and fell to the floor screaming. "It makes everything better," CC said with a satisfied expression.

Detective Towers was one of the first officers on the scene. Anne and CC watched as they took Mr. Ripley away in handcuffs. He was saying something in Bulgarian as he walked past them. CC imagined it wasn't very nice. Betsy Buttersworth came out and sat between Anne and CC on the front stairs. She put her arms around both of them. She looked at them both and then got up and went back in the house. A few minutes later, she came out with the original Phoenix glass vase. She handed it to Anne and then walked back in the house, closing and locking the door.

Chapter Fifty-Three

Sassy walked up and down the *Chicago Tribune* newspaper. The front page featured a picture of Anne and CC and a large headline that read, "Spoon Sisters Solve Murders For Sale." Sassy did not see a picture of herself. "How could there be a story without the real heroine?" She was very upset. She pawed at the newspaper and turned her head and walked away. "Bad cat," Anne said as she bent down and picked up the newspaper. She walked into the kitchen where CC was drinking her coffee and working on her blog, which now showed over 8,000 comments requesting help.

Anne flipped the paper around with a smile. "Front page, CC, front page!"

"I read the story online," CC said. "Did you see what they're calling us?"

"I think it's neat."

CC just laughed and went back to typing. "Dear Friends." She stopped and sipped her coffee. She highlighted the header that read, "From the Estate" and clicked *delete*. She typed *The Spoon Sisters, Antique Hunters.*

ABOUT THE AUTHOR

With a passion for shopping, Vicki Vass drew on her experiences as an antique hunter to tell the story of her real-life friends Anne and CC.

Vicki Vass has written more than 1,400 articles for *The Chicago Tribune* as well as *Women's World*, *The Daily Herald* and *Home & Away*. Her science fiction novel, *The Lexicon*, was inspired by her journeys in the jungle of Sudan, Africa, while writing about the ongoing civil war for World Relief.

She lives outside Chicago, with her writer, musician, husband Brian, their 20-year old son Tony, kittens Pixel and Terra, Australian shepherd Bandit, seven koi and Gary the turtle.